Riley Leonidas Hamilton

The Discoveries and Unparalleled Experience of Prof. R. Leonidas Hamilton, M.D.

with regard to the nature and treatment of diseases of the liver, lungs,

blood, and other chronic diseases

Riley Leonidas Hamilton

The Discoveries and Unparalleled Experience of Prof. R. Leonidas Hamilton, M.D.
*with regard to the nature and treatment of diseases of the liver, lungs, blood, and
other chronic diseases*

ISBN/EAN: 9783337392758

Printed in Europe, USA, Canada, Australia, Japan

Cover: Foto ©Andreas Hilbeck / pixelio.de

More available books at **www.hansebooks.com**

THE
DISCOVERIES

AND

UNPARALLELED EXPERIENCE

OF

PROF. R. LEONIDAS HAMILTON, M.D.,

WITH REGARD TO THE NATURE AND TREATMENT OF

Diseases of the Liver, Lungs, Blood.

AND

Other Chronic Diseases;

CONTAINING, ALSO,

A Biographical Sketch of His Life,

(From Harper's Magazine,)

WITH HIS

Common Sense Theory of Diseases

AND THE

Evidence of his Wonderful Cures.

☞ All Letters for Prof. Hamilton should be addressed thus:

R. L. HAMILTON, M.D.,

Post Office Box No. 4952,

New York City.

CAUTION!

I HEREBY caution the public against certain persons who have taken advantage of my extensive reputation and the wonderful efficiency of my new treatment, in palming off upon the afflicted, worthless trash of various sorts, purporting to be remedies originated and prepared by R. LEONIDAS HAMILTON, M.D. For the benefit of the public, I will say, once for all, that I DO NOT PREPARE, OR OFFER FOR SALE, IN ANY MANNER, ANY PATENT MEDICINES OR MEDICINAL PREPARATIONS OF THAT CHARACTER WHATEVER, AND I PRONOUNCE ALL SUCH COUNTERFEITS. Those who buy them do so at their peril. The only medicines I have any knowledge of are my own PRIVATE PRESCRIPTIONS, which I prepare from day to day with my own hands for those patients whom I examine and prescribe for in person or by correspondence.

PREFACE.

THE reader of this work will at once observe, that the views and theory contained in it are quite different from those usually presented by the medical profession. They are deductions and discoveries, in strict accordance with the latest developments of science; and though new to the world at large, yet they have long been entertained by me —and now I send them forth to guide the sick and suffering into the path of health and happiness. My theory and success I calmly submit to an intelligent public. Of this success I think no man can doubt, for the testimonials given of my cures are not one in a hundred of those it has been my pleasure to receive. My experience for years has proved the truth of that maxim: "Success makes success;" for it is because some sufferer has obtained relief and cure, that that sufferer has sent us another; and it is because thousands have been cured, that they have recommended to us other thousands.

I can only promise for the future what I have aimed at in the past —an exclusive, persevering and sympathizing interest to cure every patient who may apply to me. All the knowledge derived from the variety of my cases and long experience will be devoted, with entire fidelity, to the afflicted.

LIFE OF DR. HAMILTON.

The likeness of Prof. R. LEONIDAS HAMILTON, facing the title page of this little work, will be recognized as a faithful portrait by numerous patients, in every section of the country, who have visited him at his office. To thousands of other patients whom he has never seen, and who have been treated by him through the medium of correspondence, he sends this Portrait and Pamphlet, hoping it may be an acceptable reminder of him who has so often had their cases before him, through their letters, written by them when afflicted, and ever read by him with professional and personal interest, care and solicitude.

There is another class of persons who may be pleased to give these pages a perusal—THOSE IN SEARCH OF HEALTH. The sick and afflicted rightly desire to know the previous history, character and personal appearance of the Physician to whom they are about to confide the tender interests of life and health.

For the information and satisfaction of the above-named classes, and also for the gratification of the friends of the sick, and of that portion of the general public who are, or may hereafter become, interested in his Medical Discoveries and world-wide Professional Success, Prof. HAMILTON begs leave to submit the following Personal Biography. It originally appeared in that most reputable and widely circulated of all the American magazines, "*Harper's Monthly*," from the number of which for February, 1868, we copy. It is merely an outline sketch; for no one but a physician knows anything of the filling up of the life of the faithful medical man, or has any conception of the daily, unceasing, never done cares which make up the routine of his ever-active life.

From *Harper's Monthly, February*, 1868.

" We present our readers with a Biographical Sketch of one of the 'representative men,' not only of New York, but of this country. We have the evidence for saying that but few professional men are as widely known ; for he has not only medically treated thousands of the af-

flicted of every State in the American Union, but also numerous patients from all the British Colonies, Mexico, the West India Islands,
and nearly every part of Europe and the East. Prof. HAMILTON would
be a representative man were he to devote himself to the sciences in
general, or to mercantile, manufacturing or professional life. The
marked cranial development and facial expression before the reader
is one which all would recognize at once as intellectual, energetic and
executive.

"'Blood will tell,' can not be less true of man than of the horse and
the other domestic animals whose pedigrees we are so careful to con-
trol. Our race has its own aristocracy—not, in this glorious country,
always founded in wealth or attained position, but in the inherent
mental, physical or moral development of the individual—and this
individuality frequently marking a family through several generations.
Benjamin West and Vernet would have been artists had they been born
anywhere. Audubon was a naturalist, Humboldt a philosopher, Napoleon the First a man of god-like energy, and Alexander Hamilton a
statesman, by virtue of their own natural powers and gifts.

"The genealogy of R. LEONIDAS HAMILTON can be distinctly traced,
in common with that of Alexander Hamilton, to Sir David de Hamilton,
almost five hundred years ago; but whilst the immediate ancestors of
Alexander Hamilton lived in the island of Nevis, one of the West Indies, the grandfather of the subject of this sketch was among the early
settlers of the 'Old Bay State,' from whence several of his brothers removed to the central and western parts of the 'Empire State,' from
whom have sprung many representatives of the Hamilton family, several of whom are physicians of eminence and marked ability. But he
of whom we now write, and who is engaged in one of the widest hu-
manitarian enterprises of the Western Continent, owes nothing to an-
cestry, unless it be a good brain and that early poverty which compelled him, while yet a mere boy, to depend upon himself, and to brave
the world for himself. His immediate ancestors and their relatives
were men and women of marked *physique*, tall and erect, with great
activity of temperament and paramount executiveness. Dr. HAM-
ILTON's father and mother died when he was only nine years of age,
and what estate was left fell to the lawyers who settled it, and left our
hero a struggling orphan boy, and he was placed with an uncle to
serve his minority upon a farm. But his natural taste and talent now

showed itself. Medicine was his chosen and pet study. In mere boy-hood he was often sought when the neighboring farmers were sick. As soon as he had gathered a few dollars from small accumulations, in-stead of squandering it for trifles, he bought his supply of medicines and books—the former for the benefit of his friends when sick, and the latter for his own fond study. A rainy day—that only time of rest to a fatherless boy apprenticed to a farmer—always found him alone with his books and medicines, studying out some difficult case which puz-zled his brain. His studious habits and firm resolve to be a physician were opposed by his relatives, which only served as a stimulus to goad his energies on.

"But physical toil and study and discouragements wore upon both mind and body. In spite of every effort to rally his strength and courage, his stamina was soon gone. Consumption, that insidious and fatal disease, belonged to his family, and had taken away, one by one, his relatives, and now, at the early age of seventeen, his own health showed signs of rapid decline.

"He was confined to the bed for nearly six months, during which time the most eminent physicians were consulted, and all the boasted remedies for consumption were used in vain, and he was given up to die—the consumptive's death. But spring came, and its genial warmth invited him into the open air. He seemed partially to revive, and with his reviving power came the resolve to throw all medicines aside. He determined to live at any rate.

"While taking a short walk one day, a traveling physician—a Frenchman—passing by, stopped and conversed with him. He told him of remedies for his case from the adjacent fields and forests, 'with-out money and without price,' and only accepted the farmer's house-hold hospitalities. From that day strength came to him; hectic and cough left, and soon he ate with the hungry heartiness of a starved, growing boy. Hope now lighted and lightened his heart; and his new and true physician made him fully acquainted with the remedies he employed, and with their magically restorative effects. He fully re-covered, and vowed anew to devote himself to medicine. Saved, him-self, he determined to spend his life in saving the lives of his fellow-men. At the age of twenty he had read much medicine, whilst yet he was only the farmer's apprentice, and he now determined to devote himself wholly to his chosen profession. He entered the office of a physician, and afterward studied with another, who devoted his whole attention to chronic affections of the liver, lungs and blood. Still persevering, he entered a medical college, from which he graduated with such honor that he was soon invited to be Professor of Materia Medica, Therapeutics and Pharmacy, and he afterwards held the chair of Diseases of Females and Children in the same college.

" He now entered the field of active general practice of medicine and surgery; and for fifteen years few men visited more families, saw a greater variety of diseases, devoted themselves more zealously, or independently, or with more singleness of purpose, to cure his patients wherever a wide reputation called him. Especially did he investigate and pride himself upon his success in cases of incipient consumption, liver diseases and constitutional weakness—cases which other physicians dreaded, and which they declared themselves unable to cure. Here was his peculiar glory; not boastful, but gratefully thankful that he could cure those patients whose cases were like his own. He investigated medicines, especially the vegetable materia medica, with enthusiasm, and nothing afforded him so much satisfaction as to ' get just the right remedy ' for the patient who consulted him.

" After being engaged in the practice of medicine and surgery for so many years, Dr. HAMILTON's health failed to such an extent that he was compelled to relinquish the out-door, night-and-day, ever-anxious and ever-varied work of the general practitioner. His sympathies and his tastes, his experience and his success, at once determined him to make a specialty of diseases of the Lungs, Liver, and Blood, and other chronic diseases. Next, he was to decide where he could do most good—where benefit the greatest number. His discerning sagacity instantly pointed him to New York city, as the center of the Western World.

" He planned an immense medical business, and secured the most competent and eminent physicians, chemists and pharmaceutists in the Union; and all of his vast medical business is daily conducted with clock-like regularity, and every department of it is dispatched under his direct and personal supervision. Nothing passes without his sanction. No letters or correspondence are, under any circumstances, opened, except by himself.

" It is now an admitted fact that for many years past Dr. HAMILTON has made more examinations, and prescribed for more sick people, than any other man in the world. He has evidence to show this. He has devoted much time and an immense amount of money to the investigation of new medicinal agents. He examines so many thousands of cases annually, by personal examination and by correspondence, that he is enabled to decide, with the utmost skill and success, upon just the right remedies required. His treatment is no one-idea patent medicine remedy—no humbug scheme; but, from a great variety of the most choice remedies, carefully selected and compounded according to his own specific directions, he makes up each prescription from the symptoms and condition of each case of disease, as presented. The number of his patients is only limited by his ability to see them or to prescribe for them by letter.

" As the popular physician with the people of this country, he is to them what Stewart and Claflin are as dry goods merchants, or as the Harpers and Appletons and Putnams are as publishers—the representative man. Original in his reasonings, decided in his convictions, quick in his conceptions, he has done, and can do, an immense labor, accurately and successfully; and he is reaping the harvest of gratitude from patients in our own and other countries.

" As before suggested, he has remarkable enthusiasm in the investigation of medicinal agents, and has so many patients afflicted with the same class of diseases of the Liver, Lungs and Blood, at the same time, that he has the best possible opportunity to test the relative efficacy and value of remedies; and herein, perhaps, is one of the strongest features of his wonderful skill, but not by any means the only feature. His views of the nature of disease—and especially of those to which we have referred—are peculiarly his own. The conclusions arrived at from investigations made by him years since are now fully proved by others to be correct. He was only twenty years in advance of his age. His distinctive and peculiar discovery is that the liver is as important an organ, as a blood-maker and blood-purifier, as the lungs are as blood-*vitalizers*—to coin a word expressive of the oxygenation of the blood in the latter organs. It is the thorough understanding of this *specific liver function*, and of its relation to disease, and the discovery and adoption of his own peculiar remedies, which have created for him a medical world of his own. Liberal in his views of medicine, and ever happy to receive suggestions from others, his mind is so sagacious and practical that he scrutinizes with remarkable accuracy, and discriminates what is true in what comes before his active brain.   Such a man creates faith, makes success, and eminently deserves all that world-wide popularity which he has already secured, and which is promised to him in the glorious future."

The following was composed by William Ross Wallace, the celebrated poet, from hints in an elegant paper presented to Prof. HAMILTON by a committee of eminent physicians as a token of their appreciation of his noble work :

A Life Ode.

TO PROF. R. LEONIDAS HAMILTON, M. D.

BROTHER in our grand and sacred calling, not that word of ours
Can a single new addition give unto your mighty powers,
Nor that we can twine a single new leaf in the wreath of Fame,
That has grown, and still is growing, on your world-acknowledged
    name,
Do we thus, at last, address you—we who blindly did so long
War against your *certain* Healing—doing *real* Science wrong ;
Not for these we waft you greeting, but in justice to the Plan
That your Inspiration, Study, offers for the Ills of MAN !
Yes, triumphant offer, giving tens of joyous thousands Wealth,
Richer than all golden ingots, in the Eden Rose of Health ;
Health that is the great foundation for the Muscle, Mind and Heart,
Leading into every Science, giving luster to all Art.
With it only Man has *manhood*, sees his forces surely hurled
On the broad, rude breast of Matter to imparadise a world.
O, without it what's existence ?   How philosophy must die,
All unread Earth's mystic volume and Star-Libraries on high.

What the ponderous brain of Statesman ?   What the earnest Preach-
    er's fire ?
What the Patriot-Hero's saber ?   What the ardent Poet's lyre ?
What the eager man of business ?   Lashed by Fiend Disease's rod,
What to Man is Earth ?   A Desert, though so opulent made by God.
But Disease's Demon banished, how majestically he stands,
Little lower than the Angels, with sound brain and stalwart hands !

BROTHER ! those the truths so startling that you pondered long ago,
How for REMEDY you labored as you wept o'er Human woe !
How you saw the BLOOD, the *very fountain* of the Human Life ;
There it *was* that with the Demon *must* be waged the saving strife,
From the Regal Blood *all* Poison *must* be driven ; it *must* roll
Free, and *Pure*, and *Strong*, and *Steady*, as the God-protected pole.
O, how solemnly you questioned Science on her moveless throne,
" What's *Main* Purifier, Strainer of the Blood within its zone ? "

Questioned not with mere lips only, but with *conscientious* work,
Toiling bravely as a *Christian*, never dreaming as a *Turk*,
Soon you found the great *true* answer, Science opening wide her
    book.
"Earnest, Human-loving Searcher, to the *central* LIVER look,
Nor the *Lungs* discard in treatment; go *on* as you have *begun*,
And Humanity by thousands will bless NATURE's *Hamilton!*"

But the REMEDY? Not *Mineral :* it, at most, *lulls* the ill;
Even if it may cure sometimes, opens way for worse ones still;
Yes, the VEGETABLE gives it, root, and stem, and leaf, and flower,
Innocent as Eden-foliage, though so mighty in their power?
Were and are they not? Speak thousands—ye who our wise brother
    sought,
And proclaim to those yet suffering all the victory he wrought!
Tell how fled the sallow, yellow color from the skin or face—
Nature's own red roses, lilies, taking their heaven-ordered place;
Fled all Drowsiness and Dullness; bitter, bad taste in the mouth,
Frequent Headache, heat internal, and the throat's Zahara drouth ;
Fled the heart's wild palpitation ; Cough so teasing and so dry ;
Appetite unsteady, viands hateful to the taste and eye :
Sour Stomach, with a raising of the food ; and in the throat
Horrible Sensation, Choking over which a fiend would gloat ;
Heaviness of Vomiting, or Pain in sides, or back or breast ;
Colic Pain and Soreness through the heated bowels, without rest ;
Constipation of the bowels, Diarrhœa, aching Piles ;
In extremities a Coldness, deep as felt by Arctic Isles,
To the head a swift blood rushing, Female Weaknesses the worst ;
Spirits *low,* Forebodings *gloomy*, as if by black doom accursed,
Irritable and Desponding—nothing bright in all the world,
And a very nuisance, even rainbow's peace symbolic curled,
Yes, our BROTHER ! these the Miseries that your *chartered* skill has
    slain,
Not forgetting fell Consumption and her diabolic train.
BROTHER ! if we cry out "Onward" to the Chemist, to the one
Piercing down to read Earth's History, mystic daughter of the Sun,
How much more should we cry "Onward" to the *true* Physician
    —he
Who in strong but modest effort probes our great Humanity?
This Humanity still subtler than the Elemental thrall,
For it is the *Microcosm* of the Macrocosm—all !

Onward, then, in Heavenly Mission ! Onward with that piercing eye,
That can *all* Diseases Chronic in the Patient's frame descry?
Onward, with your Heart so feeling, so rejoicing to dispel
From Humanity Diseases blasphemous, usurping Hell ;
O, may *long*, LONG, LONG your Mission for our aching Race remain,
Heaven giving you the vigor still to bear the ceaseless strain
By so many myriad Sufferers forced upon a soul and frame,
To the Throne of Health devoted, with her Eden-nataled flame !

Onward, with the glad warm blessings of the myriads you save
Daily from Disease's torture—daily from the early grave ;
Blessings breathed by Mothers, Fathers, Children, Brothers, Sisters,
    all
From whose fame restored your Healing drives away the greedy pall !
Onward till a blessing holier than is vouchsafed to the sod
Glows upon you in that country far above the ailing Clod :
Blessings for the *true* physician, from the *First Physician*—GOD !

MANY PHYSICIANS.

EVIDENCE FROM THAT EMINENT POET, WM. ROSS WALLACE,
OF NEW YORK.

A Grateful Heart's Acrostic.

Proud may you be that thus you *laureled* stand,
Rich in the praises of our grateful land,
O'er which your Genius and your science save
Full many thousands, yearly from the grave !

River you *see* the very CENTRAL place,
Evermore cause within the Human Race
Of fell Disease's ill, the terrible *source*,
Not with a pigmy's spite but with a giant's force,
If it gives not the *natural* movement-flows ;
Dark and corrupt the grave-doomed system grows,
All helpless as an eagle, nearing death,
Succumbed beneath a Simoon's poison-breath.

Hold you the *mineral* antidote ? *It* kills,
And only *faster* death's black stillness fills.
" Mankind," you cried, " *Another* power must find ;
In something *else* is *final* Rescue shrined.
Lo, in the *Vegetable*, HEALTH'S FROM GOD ;
To it *alone* breaks the Destroyer's rod ! "
O, *I* do KNOW your blest, triumphant skill,
Now, *saved* by *you* from his Demoniac Will !

May you long live, more lives thus to prolong ;
Day after day the *Proof* how true this *grateful* song !

DEAR DOCTOR, at 546 Broadway : When I felt myself cured by
your truly great skill, working under your true system of medicine,
I saw that my avowal of my intention to show my gratitude in " A
Rhyme," was received by you as a *passing* ejaculation of joy ; but

I was *in earnest*, and I only regret that the necessary shortness of an acrostic prevents me from stating details of your triumphs, in which record would be made of your *full* success in ridding thousands on thousands, of scores of diseases caused by derangement of the Liver. My little lyric is sent to you as a matter of bounden duty as well as pleasure. God bless you for exertions in your sacred profession.   W.

Inventors and Specialists—How Progress is Made.

This is an age of discovery. In all the annals of history there is no period described when there were so many and so valuable inventions. A few years since we all traveled in stage coaches, six or eight miles an hour; now cars, some of which are miniature parlors, carry us swifter than race-horses on the track, and steamboats transport us to distant cities, during our sleep, in a single night. Two inventors—Stevenson, of England, and Fulton, of our own country—have accomplished most of this for us. A few years since, our feet were kept dry only by soaking our clumsy boots with tallow; while now, both the most substantial and most fastidious tastes can be satisfied with excellent and elegant foot-coverings of rubber; and a Goodyear has perfected its manufacture in a hundred utensils and conveniences, for the kitchen, the parlor, the nursery, and the study. The genius of Morse has invented the telegraph, and the messages of commerce, news, legislation, and friendship sweep over the magic wires with lightning speed. Not many years since, the greatest of living surgeons, Velpeau, of Paris, told his medical pupils that although enthusiasts at different times had vainly imagined that some means might be adopted to allay the pain of surgical operations, yet that such an idea was entirely chimerical and must ever remain so. The thing, he said, was impossible, and all hopes of it but a vain delusion. In five years from that hour, Velpeau amputated limbs, and performed other grave operations, whilst his willing patient was sleeping from anæsthesia. An American dentist, Dr. Horace Wells, of Hartford, Conn., conceived the idea of preventing the pain of surgical operations, and first of all took the ether himself, to have a tooth extracted. He devoted years to this discovery, with an enthusiasm not excelled among ancient or modern inventors or discoverers.

Such are a few of the marks of mighty progress in a few years of the past. Who made these discoveries? Always and ever, ENTHUSI-ASTS and SPECIALISTS. Never has the world seen men more devoted to single, definite, specific objects. Stevenson and Fulton loved the steam-engine, the steam-car and the steamboat, with all the devotion that Napoleon loved the victories of war, or St. Paul the contests for the faith on Mars' Hill. Day and night, year after year, did the ever-to-be-honored Goodyear, in alternate prosperity, poverty, and prison, develop his invaluable discoveries. So with Morse. So with every discoverer and inventor. Opposition, old theories, all the knowledge of the past, were opposed to each and every one of them. Electricians and chemists thought Morse was a fool; surgeons and professors ridiculed Wells; and almost the whole lives of Stevenson and Fulton were met with obloquy and contempt. Goodyear was imprisoned for debt, and Dr. Wells was so disheartened by ingratitude that he died in prison by his own hands! These men were SPECIALISTS, and as such were denounced as enthusiasts and humbugs and deceivers; but the world will honor them, whilst their opponents will be lost in ignoble nothingness and absolute forgetfulness.

Just so in medicine. Jenner devoted years to the discovery and investigation of vaccination, whilst his medical brethren arrayed themselves against him in united hatred.

From these facts—and they are only a few among many that might be adduced—we should learn :

1st. That no man can excel who does not devote his whole ener-gies to some one, definite, determined object.

2d. That such men are always either slighted or opposed by those in the same employment or profession.

8d. That those discoveries which look the most chimerical are often the most reliable and valuable, and their authors the greatest benefac-tors of their race.

4th. That there is a want of faith which is foolish. Once nobody thought these men were wise; now every person of sense sees at a glance that these persons were, each and all, a hundred years in ad-vance of their age. The world is full of doubters and sneerers; but the true discoverer should never regard their conduct, but press on to the brightest attainments—that he may acquire honor to himself and bless mankind.

The True Theory of Chronic Diseases.

WHY ARE WE DISEASED?

Sickness is not the natural condition of the human family. Man, infinitely raised above all other animals, by his intelligence, his moral capacities, and his immortal life, suffers more from disease than all other animals. In fact, sickness seems á stranger to all the beasts of the field, the birds of the air, and to the sportive swimmers in the brooks, lakes and oceans. We have only the rarest evidence of disease among the inferior animals. Whenever the domestic animals—our horses, sheep, swine, and cattle—are sick, we can almost always ascribe it to the wrongs done to them by man in respect to diet, exposure or hardships.

But how common is sickness to our race! From the cradle to the grave we are constantly liable to it. Indeed, the best writers on hygienic and medical topics concede that more than one-half of all our race die before they are three years old! From the cradle to the grave our bodies are halting hospitals for the frequent residence of disease.

The average period of human life may have increased within the past fifty years, because the treatment of disease has improved, and neither men nor infants are butchered by blood-letting and depressing, strength-destroying and poisonous remedies, as formerly; but who will say that the American people are now as strong as were the fathers and mothers of the period of the Revolution! Children were far healthier, and men and women were larger and stronger. Dyspepsia was very rare, consumption scarcely heard of, and neuralgia unknown.

Twenty-five years ago the greatest number of deaths were produced by fevers and inflammation. To-day five persons die from some disease arising from impure blood, or dyspepsia, or exhausted nervous debility, or consumption, where one dies from fever. The race is smaller, more sickly and sensitive, and have neither the buoyancy, contentedness, nor strength of those who lived in the days of our fathers and mothers. Every man of experience, and every nurse of goodly years, will testify to what we say, and every physician knows it to be abundantly true.

Why is all this? The race has changed its climate. Our ancestors came from England, Ireland, Scotland, France, Germany; and the climate there was different. The countries named had a less varied temperature, and there are comparatively no malarial influences there. Our country is, in almost all sections and at almost all seasons, exceedingly variable as to the temperature and humidity of its atmosphere. To-day it is cool and dry, and to-morrow it is chilly and wet, to-day it is hot and dry, and to-morrow it is foggy and sweltering, or chilly, wet, and raw. The soil, too, is new, and its newly upturned soil exhales the depressing and blood poisonous influences of malaria. Vegetable decay, and chilly moisture, and sudden changes of the weather, produce internal congestions, and, more than all, they develop those bilious affections which prevail in every section of the country. Who is not bilious? Who does not have a torpid or diseased liver?

Liver, Lung, and Blood Diseases.

Dr. HAMILTON wishes it distinctly understood that his discoveries in reference to the above diseases have not all been made in a single month or year. Twenty-five years of unceasing labor have been devoted to the daily observation, study and treatment of the above diseases, and those other chronic diseases which are mostly caused by them. During this time more than two hundred and eight thousand patients have been under his professional care and treatment. A very large proportion of these have been treated by letter. Some may suppose that a physician could not obtain a sufficiently accurate view of the condition of a sick person by correspondence to treat them successfully. My experience proves otherwise; for some of the most remarkable cures of the worst cases have been conducted through the medium of letter-writing. In most chronic (or long-continued) cases the patient has thought over his own symptoms hundreds of times. He has noticed the location of every pain, the time at which he was most subject to it, and whether acute or mild, constant or occasional, and under what circumstances he was subject to it. He has often observed whether he was feverish or chilly, whether he had rush of blood to the head, with or without chilliness of the hands and feet; and he knows whether he is full of blood and plethoric, or is pale and bloodless; and he always states these matters with common sense and accuracy when writing to me; for he has a very good, if not a professional, appreciation of the whole subject of the circulation of the blood in his case. Just so in regard to digestion. He always states whether food distresses him, whether troubled with acidity or wind in the stomach, what kind of food agrees with him, whether his tongue is bilious and coated, and his mouth troubled with bad tastes, or is clean and healthy; and gives such other facts as lead the physician to intelligently and reliably diagnose the actual condition of the digestive system.

Patients Know More than the Doctors Think.

The people are far more intelligent in these matters than physicians suppose, or are willing to allow. Every person of ordinary intelligence understands that a coated tongue, bad breath, bad taste in the mouth, headache, and sometimes nausea, pain or wind in the stomach, indicate a morbid condition of the stomach and liver. They do not understand precisely in what that condition consists, but they express it all in that word—everywhere known—"bilious." Both the stomach and liver are subject to numerous diseases, which none but the man who has studied the structure and functions and diseases of these organs can correctly understand; but the great difficulty among almost all physicians in these cases is that they do not use the right remedies. Castor oil, rhubarb, seidlitz powders, soda, magnesia, quinine, gentian, bismuth, blue mass and calomel make up the great list of their remedies for all chronic diseases of the stomach and liver! A list of agents this, which is nauseous enough to make any man sick, and poisonous enough to forever keep him sick!

The people know their symptoms and their sufferings, but they know not their diseases, nor where to go for relief. They write out their symptoms just as they feel them, and have felt them for months, whether those symptoms refer to the circulation or the lungs, or the brain and the spinal system, or the kidneys or other organs.

We have often noticed another feature: When a physician is examining a patient, that patient is often confused. The sufferer gives wrong answers or imperfect answers ; or, after the physician has left, the patient finds that he has forgotten to give one half of the true symptoms. Not so in writing. The patient, or an intelligent friend, states just what their sufferings and feelings are, without being embarrassed at all. When he has written it all down, he looks his letter over again, and sees whether he has omitted any thing, or incorrectly stated any of his feelings, pains or other matters. And so it is true, entirely true, that the physician will often get a more exact view of his patient's case by a letter than by a personal questioning and careful " cross-examination " of his patient. In a letter the patient is entirely confidential and true to nature in expressing the symptoms. The timid, suffering lady speaks just as she feels and just as she suffers ; and one great reason why we have so well succeeded in intricate and delicate diseases of the nervous system, of the heart, of the liver, of the kidneys, uterus and bladder, when, perhaps, the visiting physician has entirely failed, has been because the confusion and timidity of the lady prevented her from giving that *natural* statement of her case to her physician which she could write, and did write to us in her letters. Many such letters are more perfect photographs of disease than can be found in the most elaborate and pains-taking medical works of French, German and English authors.

Letters Speak the Truth.

Patients know that all these letters to me are strictly confidential, and not made the neighborhood talk through the "blabbing doctor" of their village. And from such unreserved and perfectly natural letters I have very often been led to detect some obscure valvular disease of the heart, of which they little dreamed; or some bilious caluli in the gallduct that never had been surmised by their usual physician; or some fatal kidney disease that was, all unknown to them, pouring off the vital forces of life ; or some obscure womb disease, from which the victim had suffered for months; or some poison of the blood, inherited or unknowingly caught, of which the patient had not the slightest idea ! Hundreds of such have been cured by us, who would otherwise have died; and whose disease would have forever remained unknown, unless the physician should have discovered it by an examination after death! What an idea! To die without our disease being known, and die *because* our disease was not known!

Our Experience of Written Symptoms.

It requires no little experience to judge of the contents of such letters correctly. What is necessary is for the patients to state their exact feelings. Many symptoms which to them seem important are frequently not so, but our experience leads us to discriminate. There is a tact in this which science cannot teach, nor man define. And yet the man who has a natural and instinctive talent will discern, as if by some unseen agency, the seat of the disease, and have the intuitive sagacity to apply the right remedy.

How many hours, months and years we have thus spent in reading letters from our patients! No hand but my own ever opens these letters, and no other eyes are permitted to see their contents if the case be confidential. What mirrors of human suffering! What records of pains and griefs! What pictures of every disease to which humanity is subject! Is it any marvel that we seize the significant symptoms, and interpret rightly from what our patient, whose letter is before us, is suffering? Is it any wonder that, with an intuitive glance, we scan both the manifest disease, and also the secret enemy, of which the patient knows nothing? If we did not, we should be destitute of that instinctive sagacity which makes nature's true physician. Can you read the very inner thoughts of a friend by the expression of his countenance, when he knows not that you are even looking at him? and shall not we be able, by both science and natural insight, to divine how and from what you suffer? And after so long an experience, is it any wonder that, ever questioning closely the records of science and the daily open book of disease in the patients before us, we should have made DISCOVERIES as to disease! Years ago an intuitive apprehension of great truths was opened to us, even before we ever taught, as a Professor in a Medical College, the facts of medical science. And as the great naturalist, Humboldt, learned the aspects of nature by traveling in every clime and every country, so we must suppose that we have seen almost every feature of chronic disease to which the human system is subject. There is no county or city, or scarcely a village in all the mighty domain of our vast country, which is not the home of one, or several, of our patients. Our increasing observation only strengthened the suggestions of our instinctive views in regard to those causes of disease which make up the great mass of human suffering.

———

Diseases Caused by Liver Complaint.

These are most frequent and universally prevalent. Why is this? Let us use common sense and look at this matter:

The human system, the most perfect of all the works of the creator, is so constituted that, to be entirely healthy, it must throw off the waste, worn-out and poisonous materials as fast as it takes on new materials from our food and drink. The food is assimilated and made into nourishing and healthy blood, principally through the offices of the stomach, liver and lungs. The worn-out materials are mostly excreted by the liver, lungs and kidneys; but all medical men have heretofore failed to recognize the vast importance of the liver as a blood-purifying and excreting organ. The most learned German physiologists, who base their assertions upon actual experiments only, state that the amount of BILE which should be manufactured by the liver and poured into the intestines each day is two and one-half pounds. All persons interested to know this fact and the experiments to prove it may consult *Verdaungssaefte und Stoffwechsel*, Leipzig, 1852; or they may see a *resume* of these facts in Prof. Dalton's Physiology.

Remember one thing more: The bile is something more than the natural physic of the bowels, as has heretofore been taught by eminent medical men. The bile is mostly made up of the waste matter, of the blood—effete, worn-out and injurious materials. If the liver does not make this bile and pour it into the intestines daily, it remains in the blood as a poison. It poisons the blood itself, and circulates, as irritating and poisonous matter in the blood, to every organ in the system.

The blood poisoned with the daily accumulated excess of bile, returns from the liver to the heart, and the nerves of the heart are affected, and we have an oppressed feeling at the heart, and palpitation;

and if this cause is long continued we get chronic irritation, undue excitement, and morbid nutrition of the heart, developing many forms of Heart Disease.

Just so with the LUNGS. The bile-poisoned blood goes from the upper and right cavity of the heart to the lower cavity, and thence directly to the lungs, circulating all through those most delicate organs. The lung tissues are poisoned and irritated, and they invite the scrofulous humors of the blood, because they are thus irritated. Hence Consumption, which is local scrofula, so defined and proved by *Lugol*, and all the most scientific authors. The lungs try to oxygenize and purify the blood, and they do it in a great measure, but they are overworked and irritated, and you smell the blood-poison matters in the man's foul breath. Catarrh, Bronchitis, Asthma, Nervous Cough and Consumption itself are the results. If the Liver had done its duty, made and excreted that BILE, the Lungs would not have been diseased.

Just so with the BLOOD itself. It goes from the lungs back to the upper left cavity of the heart, thence to the lower cavity, and thence through the arteries and capillaries to every organ and tissue of the system. Among the most important of those organs is the kidneys, furnishing the urinary secretion—a most important excretion. But the kidneys themselves are irritated and congested by the presence of the bile-poisoned blood—and they become diseased. Every person who has had a liver disease, knows that the urine is scanty, high-colored, and loaded with red deposits, at times, or other diseased products. Hence, diseases not only of the kidney, but also of the bladder.

But this is not all—far from it. The poisonous blood goes also from the heart to the BRAIN, and affects the great electrical center of all vitality; and the brain, stimulated by unhealthy blood, cannot perform its office healthfully. The person has dullness, headache, incapacity to keep his mind on a subject, cannot remember, has a crowded and dizzy feeling, is sleepy, becomes nervous, gloomy, easily irritated, and often has a bilious or a neuralgic headache.

And the BLOOD itself becomes diseased, and as it forms the sweat upon the surface of the skin, it is so irritating and poisonous that the person has discolored brown spots, pimples, blotches, and other eruptions, sores, boils, carbuncles, and scrofulous tumors.

Disease of the LIVER itself is the most common of all diseases. The sudden changes of the New England climate, the malarial influences of the West, and the heat also of the South, as well as the dietetic habits of the people of this country, and other causes, all tend to develop the Liver disease, in some of its varied forms, throughout the United States. This is true, both of man and beast; as every butcher knows that he finds the livers of cattle, sheep and swine diseased ten times, where he finds any other organ diseased once. Almost every person is *bilious* at some time, and many are constantly bilious. It may be mere congestion of the liver, and torpidity of its function, or this may result in some structural or organic affection. But the Liver can never be diseased without affecting the stomach, bowels, and the other organs we have spoken of, and costiveness, piles, dropsy, dyspepsia, diarrhœa and impoverished blood are among the necessary results.

By years of research, and that practical experience which is the result of testing his treatment in so many thousands of cases Dr HAMILTON is able so to treat all those diseases which result from Liver Complaint, with remedies which will strike at the root of them as by magic. There is no such word as fail in his treatment. By them the Liver and Stomach are speedily changed to an active, healthy state, the appetite regulated and restored, the blood and secretions thoroughly purified and enriched, and the whole system renovated and built up new.

Symptoms of Liver Complaint.

A sallow or yellow-color of the skin, or yellowish-brown spots on the face and other parts of the body ; dullness and drowsiness, with frequent headache ; bitter or bad taste in the mouth, dryness of the throat, and internal heat ; palpitation of the heart; a dry, teasing cough, with sore throat ; unsteady appetite ; sour stomach, with a raising of the food, and a choking sensation in the throat ; sickness and vomiting; distress, heaviness or a bloated or

*full feeling about the stomach and sides, often attended
with pains and tenderness; aggravating pains in the sides,
back or breast, and about the shoulders ; colic pain and soreness through the bowels, with heat ; constipation of the
bowels, alternating with frequent attacks of diarrhœa ;
piles, flatulence, nervousness, coldness of the extremities ;
rush of blood to the head, with symptoms of apoplexy ;
numbness of the limbs, especially at night ; cold chills,
alternating with hot flashes ; kidney and urinary difficulties ; low spirits, unsociability and gloomy forebodings.*

———

The Reason Why !

WHY IS DR. HAMILTON SUCCESSFUL?

1st.—Because he has studied these diseases for a LIFE-TIME—first becoming interested by his own sufferings.

2d.—Because he has investigated every remedy known to science, and in addition he has new remedies, unknown to the world, which were discovered and developed by himself.

3d.—Because he has no routine way of treating all cases alike, but treats each patient who sacredly commits his health to him, according to the ACTUAL CONDITION OF THAT PATIENT.

4th.—Because, having made a SPECIALTY of Liver, Lung, and Blood Diseases, he has an experience which has extended to tens of thousands of cases—a greater experience, it is safe to say, THAN ANY OTHER LIVING MAN.

5th.—Because he selects his remedies for each case with such care, uses harmless vegetable agents, and devotes his whole life and energies to making his practice successful—to get his patients THOROUGHLY AND PERMANENTLY CURED.

Synopsis.

For greater convenience of those wishing to write me about their diseases, I insert the following, which embraces nearly all that I require to know in most cases :

Have you constipation of the bowels?
Have you attacks of diarrhœa?
Have you pains in the back, sides, or shoulders?
Have you a pain or tenderness about the stomach?
Have you a dry, teasing cough?
Have you a sallow or yellow skin?
Have you brown spots on your face or any part of the body
Have you a headache?
Are you dull, heavy, or sleepy?
Have you a bitter or bad taste in the mouth?
Have you an irritation or dryness in the throat?
Have you cold chills or hot flashes ?
Have you palpitation of the heart
Is your appetite unsteady?
Is your stomach sour?
Do you raise or spit up your food?
Have you any choking spells?
Are you troubled with sickness and vomiting ?
Do you feel bloated about the stomach?
Have you a tired or sore feeling on rising in the morning?
Do you have colic pains ?
Have you wind in the stomach or bowels?
Have you piles or fistula?
Have you nervous and all-gone feelings?
Have you cold feet and hands?
Have you a rush of blood to the head ?
Have you uneasiness on lying on the sides ?
Have you fainting or epileptic fits ?
Have you great lowness of spirits?
Have you gloomy forbodings?
Is there any sediment in your urine ; if so, is it red or white?

Consumption.

What is consumption? Tubercular consumption is a disease of the lungs, produced by impure blood. The highest authorities recognize this and demonstrate it. The old theory that it is a local inflammation, to be treated with bleeding, blisters and tartar emetic, is the most cruel humbug ever put forth under the sanction of medical authority. Consumption itself is not so often hereditary as has been supposed, but that a condition of low vitality may be transmitted from parents to children is unquestionably true. It is this deficiency of vitality which is inherited—a weakness which makes nutrition imperfect, and leads to the deposit of tubercles But thousands of persons, born with feeble vitality, and who grow from infancy to youth, would never develop the consumption if the functions of the system were kept correct. But when the stomach performs its office only partially, and the food is but half digested, nothing is done to establish vitality and keep up the supply of good blood, and nourish all the tissues of the system healthfully And when the liver but imperfectly pours off the wasted, poisonous materials of the blood, through the secretion of bile, these poisonous materials are retained in the blood, and irritate every tissue of the system. How speedily does the torpid or diseased liver break down the general strength, and make the person feel languid, and weak, and faint, and drowsy, and confused! How soon does it create pain in the right side, both in the region of the liver, and a sympathetic pain in the shoulders, and spine, and through the lungs. How soon the patient has a dry, hacking cough—that "liver cough!" The lungs are irritated by the liver-poisoned blood, and the tubercles are produced, minute at first, and perhaps existing for months all unknown to their victim.

The ordinary treatment of consumption does nothing to remove tubercles To cure consumption, there is no rational way except to purify the blood. The liver must be excited to action, by the very best agents, so as to make it throw off those poisonous materials which are causing the tubercles. Other medicines may be given, to nourish the system and support vitality, and thus prevent the development of the tubercles; but it is perfectly vain to cure consumption without restoring the action of the liver. Restore the liver, remove the blood poison, relieve the cough, correct all the secretions and purify the blood, and you strike at the root of incipient consumption, and cure the patient.

We know all this from our own personal experience. We know what it is to lie on a sick bed for months, with that hacking, distressing cough. *We have been there!*

We know what cured us, and we know what has cured thousands of others. We remember hundreds of cases of catarrh, bronchitis, and consumption which have yielded to the same remedies. To the action of those remedies we have given an amount of observation never given to any other remedies, as we suppose, by any other practitioner. This will not seem extravagant to any person, even to the most intelligent physician, who knows the number of our patients. In fact we often treat the members of the physician's own family, entirely unknown to the personal friends and acquaintances of that physician. The truth is just this: most physicians do not profess to have skill in curing consumption.

We have cured, in hundreds of instances, in numerous cases, too, where both lungs were affected. In not a few cases after the patient had hectic, night-sweats, and tubercular abscesses; and these grateful patients are the persons who have sent so many thousand others to us. Consumption is, in general practice, much oftener cured than is generally supposed; many of the profession are aware of this, and this fact is now noticed in all the best works on this disease. We call the attention of the reader to a case illustrative of this fact, and ask your thoughtful consideration of it. It should interest every person who has the consumption! In the Proceedings of the Connecticut Medical Society, for 1868, page 145, may be found: "Observations, Ante-mortem and Post-mortem, upon the Case of the late President Day, by Professor S. G. Hubbard, M. D., New Haven." From this article we learn that the late Jeremiah Day, LL. D., for twenty-nine years President of Yale College, was a victim whilst a mere youth to pulmonary consumption. Mr. Day was born in Washington, Conn., August 2, 1773, and during his infancy and boyhood his vitality was feeble. He entered Yale College as a student in 1789, "but was soon obliged to leave college on account of a pulmonary difficulty, which was, doubtless, the incipient stage of the organic disease of the lungs which subsequently developed itself." He remained in feeble health for two years, and then returned to college, and graduated in 1795,

His lung difficulties were quite severe for the next six years, and he repeatedly bled from the lungs in large quantities; but in 1803 he had so far recovered as to accept a professorship, which he held until 1817, when he was chosen president, which office he held until 1836 without serious disturbance of health.

President Day died, from "old age," August 27, 1867, aged 94 years!! Why did not consumption kill him? Because he changed his physician, and was cured by altering his treatment, from being bled and blistered and starved, to a treatment of nutritious food, blood-nourishing medicines, and tonics. Did he have the consumption? Both lungs were involved to a large extent, and a considerable portion of the lung structure was ulcerated and spit off, and large cavities were formed in both lungs.

What is the positive evidence of this? We will give this in the language of Professor Hubbard, who, in speaking of the examination of the lungs after death, says, in the article just referred to, p. 149:

" On opening the thorax, only a moderate quantity, perhaps a pint, of serum was found in both cavities—THE LUNGS WERE EVERYWHERE FREE FROM TUBERCULAR DEPOSIT, AND IN ALL RESPECTS HEALTHY. In the apex of each lung, however, was found a dense, corrugated, circular cicatrix, an inch and a half or more in diameter; also a *third* circular cicatrix, on the left side of the left lung, a few inches below the apex, each involving such a depth of tissue as to indicate that the vomicæ, [cavities] of which they were the remains, HAD BEEN LARGE AND OF LONG DURATION. Both lungs were slightly adherent at the apex.

Prof. Hubbard further remarks, most truthfully:

" Here then, was all that remained to mark the beginning, progress, and cure of a case of tubercular consumption, occupying *twelve years* in its period of activity, and with its incipient stage dating back more than *three-quarters of a century.* A legible record, surpassing in interest and importance to the human race. those of the slabs of Nineveh. or the Runic inscriptions."

Cases like the above are constantly occurring in our practice, so far as curing consumption is concerned. We could fill many pages with them, but President Day was so widely known, and lived so long, after *both* lungs had been extensively diseased, and died with lungs "*in all respects* healthy," that his case must be conclusively satisfactory. But we do not ask the reader to rest the evidence on what has been done by *other* physicians for *their* patients.

Diseases of the Blood.

SCROFULA, SALT RHEUM, OLD SORES, ERYSIPELAS, ACNE, BOILS AND CARBUNCLES.

In some cases there seems to be proof, from our most careful observation, that these humors are hereditary—acquired from one or both of the parents. But in a far greater number it is not so. They are developed as the result of liver-poison. Correct the biliary system, and give such sanitive vegetable alteratives as purify the diseased blood, and these diseases vanish as if by magic.

"The Blood is the Life." This is as true as a mathematical or any other scientific proposition; and it is a truth which should influence every physician. For no physician can excel in this class of diseases unless he makes a special, thorough, long-continued study of those vegetable remedies which purify the blood. Here, we claim, is one of our most signal triumphs—HAVING DISCOVERED, BY MOST THOROUGH RESEARCH AND INVESTIGATION, THOSE PLANTS WHICH PURIFY THE BLOOD.

These diseases cause years of unhappiness, disappointment, and suffering; and persons suffering from any bad humor are exceedingly liable to have it settle on the lungs, or some other vital organ. It is always a safe rule, and it is the only safe one for such persons, to remove the disease at once, before the blood-poison has fastened upon the heart, lungs, or kidneys. When you purify the blood and cure salt-rheum, you not only cure the salt-rheum, but you put the system in such an improved condition that you are not so liable to any disease! Cleanse the fountains of life, and good digestion, a fair skin, buoyant spirits, and vital strength will all return to you.

We have scarcely had more grateful letters than those from many of our lady patients, in both city and country, who have written to thank us for curing those eruptions of the face which are so common —acne.

Many of the impurities of the blood arise from diseases which it would not be right to discuss in a pamphlet like this, designed for circulation in the families of our country. The impure diseases of large cities have received from us no small show of attention; and we can treat those symptoms of secondary and tertiary disease, just as well for patients at a distance as for those who present themselves at our office.

Even slight affections of this character are often the source of much mortification and disappointment, and canker many a life which might otherwise be happy. Write us confidentially, so we shall know just what to do for you, and all will be well!! Very frequently persons suffer from this class of affections who do not dream of it until they write us their symptoms. "A word to the wise is sufficient." Remember to procure a remedy in season which shall eradicate every taint of impurity.

We cannot give certificates in all these classes of cases, because to do so would violate professional confidence—a point dearer than life to the physician of honor.

Diseases of the Heart.

We have referred to the fact that impure blood, filled with irritating, poisonous materials, often affects the delicate tissues of the heart. These diseases of the heart are many of them only nervous, and frequently arise sympathetically from disease of the stomach or liver; but though only nervous at first, they are liable to produce irritation and inflammation of the valves and lining membranes of the heart itself. How wise to attend to a case of this kind in season. How wise to be admonished, by the unnatural throbbing of that organ, that all is not right! How wise to be warned by that pain which you feel through the heart, that you should help it to beat rightly and to give you continued life, by your taking such medicines as shall preserve it from further disease. Purify the blood and remove the irritation at once. Patients who have suffered from heart difficulties for months and years, are often surprised to realize how soon all their troubles are removed. We give no poisons to corrupt the blood, but prescribe those blood-purifying plants which an all-wise Providence has distributed in every field and meadow and forest. Our country is rich, it would seem, above all other countries, in the number and variety of these medical plants; and to the study of such agents we have devoted a vast botanical and therapeutic investigation. Some physicians who devote much attention to the nature of heart diseases are entirely unsuccessful in their treatment. They *have not the right remedies.* Other diseases are often produced by heart diseases. Some disease of the brain frequently results from heart disease. The lungs are often diseased, by the same cause; and dropsy is often caused by the organic heart diseases. Apply in season, before the disease has become too seated.

Diseases of the Kidneys and Bladder.

Remember that urine is always formed directly from the blood—never directly from what we drink. It is simply and solely a secretion made from the blood, which goes to the kidneys; but it is a most important secretion. Many persons suffering from diseases of the kidneys are entirely unaware of it. Sometimes they are doctored for months for other diseases, when the real seat of difficulty is the kidneys. We have often treated such cases. Not unfrequently, the patient gets very much emaciated, and his strength mostly gone, before he applies to us. But his own *natural* statement of his feelings, and of the character of his urine, has enlightened us at once, and he has been saved by remedies which purified his blood, acted magically upon his liver, and stayed the wasting disease.

Patients who suffer a dull or severe pain in the back, above the hips and at each side of the spine, should look to it at once and not neglect it. If there be tenderness on pressure at the place above named, with too profuse or too scanty urine, these symptoms should attract your attention at once. If there be cloudy flakes, or red, "brick-dust" deposit in the urine, no time should be lost. If it curdles into flakes when you heat a little of it, or add a little nitric acid to it, you had better be restored from such a condition as soon as possible. Resort to nature's remedies at once, before the kidney is destroyed in its structure.

No person, unacquainted with the structure, functions and diseases of the kidneys, can rightly estimate the importance of their healthy action. If they do not act rightly, the rheumatism may be rapidly developed, or the person is liable to be suddenly attacked with dropsy, or the most aggravated and prostrating diseases of the nervous system may set in. Patients should have no hesitation in speaking confidentially, when writing us on these things. By so doing, they will enable us to discriminate, with scientific accuracy, the nature of their individual case, and aid us to choose just the right remedy to cure them.

Most of the diseases of the bladder originate from those of the kidneys. The urine is imperfectly manufactured in the kidneys, and proves irritating to the bladder and urinary passages. There is no tendency, or but very seldom any, of the diseased bladder to become cured without treatment. In nine cases out of ten, restore the action of the liver fully, and both the kidneys and bladder will be restored. When we remember that no medical agent ever reaches the kidneys, except through the liver, and the general circulation of the blood, you will see that our treatment is rational, philosophical, and scientific. We have, indeed, discovered agents which act with much direct effect upon the kidneys, healing these organs and re-establishing their functional action ; but we use them in connection with our own discovered agents for powerfully and kindly acting on the liver, and cleansing the blood from every impurity.

Many of these diseases are of a private nature, and sometimes when the patient does not suspect it. Be frank in all your statements, and assist us to understand your case, that we may cure you thoroughly.

———

Dropsy.

We have but few words to say to patients on this subject. That this disease primarily originates in liver diseases, or impure blood, or heart disease, or kidney disease, is well understood by the profession. The nature of this disease is very different, in different cases. But let the disease arise from whatever cause it may, our treatment has been eminently successful. We do not cure all cases of it, for patients sometimes neglect to apply to us until the gravest organic diseases of the liver, or heart, or kidneys complicate the case. But if any thing will "strike at the root" of the case, it is our remedies. We cannot illustrate the nature of dropsy to the readers of this pamphlet, as we would desire to, for, to understand it, requires a thorough knowledge of anatomy, physiology, and pathology, which the general reader is never supposed to have. Dropsy is one of the most intricate and interesting of all diseases. Our special success in its treatment, is owing to the fact that we use remedies which are different from the remedies usually tried by any school of medicine. To a large extent, our several remedies are original, and in their combination they are most powerful agents to cure the dropsy. There is now no section of the United States in which we have not cured cases of dropsy.

Piles.

How common is this disease! How few physicians permanently cure it! Costiveness is the most frequent and universal of all chronic diseases. It is an affection peculiar to no particular section of our country, for it prevails everywhere ; it is peculiar to no age, for it affects patients of every age ; it is peculiar to neither the robust nor the invalid, for many who otherwise enjoy (for the time being, at least) the very best of health, and three-fourths of those invalids who suffer from chronic disease, are habitually troubled with constipation ; torpid liver and imperfect secretion of bile are the great causes of this affection, and in no section of the world is it so universal as in the United States. We remove it, by removing *its cause*. We give no drastic and weakening purgatives, but only mild ones, and such as will restore a natural action of the bowels.. Nor do we rely on these for a permanent cure, but we cure permanently by restoring fully the deficient action of that " great housekeeper " of our health, the LIVER. No physician, or other man of sense, will question that this is the true and natural way. Hence our own unparalleled success ! Hence the title which the American people have everywhere given to us— " The LIVER, LUNG, AND BLOOD DOCTOR." PILES are, in nine cases out of ten, produced by costiveness ; but occasionally they are produced by disease of the liver, without costiveness. The congestion of the blood-vessels of the lower bowel, which constitutes the essence of this disease, is owing to obstruction in the return of the venous blood to the liver, and this obstruction is almost universally caused by functional or organic disease of the liver. Most physicians understand the nature and cause of this disease. Why, then, do they not cure it? Because they generally apply local treatment only—they doctor the *effect*, but let alone the *cause*. Or, if they act upon the liver, they give calomel or blue mass, which never permanently re-establishes the functions of the liver, but makes the patient still more dependent upon using, again and again, these irritating, poisonous, and life-destroying medicines. Medical men should know better than this, for they ought to learn better from their want of success. But they seem to be utterly deficient of that enterprise and originality, which distinguishes so many professional men and intelligent mechanics in other departments of labor. With most of them it is calomel or blue pill, live or die !! The treatment by simply aperient mixtures and pills is a little better. But this does not remove the cause. Agents must be given, if we would thoroughly cure the piles, which arouse the vital action of the liver, and so invigorate its action that it will be permanent. For the time being, it is also useful to use local treatment to the piles themselves, because it gives relief, and aids the speedy cure; but the only agents which permanently cure the piles are those which safely, surely and permanently restore the liver to its natural functional action.

Nervous and Sick Headache, and Neuralgia.

These affections are produced, in almost every instance, by derangement of the digestive organs and liver disease. It is rare, indeed, that a person who has good digestion, and is not costive, and who has a proper action of the liver, suffers from any form of headache or neuralgia. The great deficiency in the usual medical treatment is, that the medicines which are given to correct the bowels, do not have any permanent action on the liver. The cathartic medicines will give relief for a time, but they do not remove the cause. There is another mistake in the usual treatment. It is not true that the headache is altogether caused by the present state of the liver and bowels. The truth is, that by reason of the imperfect action of the liver, the blood has not been properly purified, and it is this impure blood circulating through the system, and coming in contact with the delicate nerve tissue of the brain, which is also a very prominent and constant cause of the headache. The same is true of neuralgia. It almost always exists in connection with impure blood, or else with blood which is deficient in red globules. Our treatment strikes the root. It re-establishes the action of the liver, and produces such a state, that it keeps up a normal or healthy action; and our treatment also purifies and enriches the blood.

There are also numerous other conditions of the nervous system, besides neuralgia and headache, to which the same remarks are applicable, and which are cured speedily and permanently by our remedies.

Rheumatism.

Under this general head we will say a few words to patients afflicted with this disease, and with other diseases which frequently accompany it. By referring to our testimonials of cures of this disease, the reader will observe how quickly and surely our remedies have acted. Reader, is your case any worse than some of those given in these certificates? If not, there certainly is hope for you. Remember, that all these cases are but a few of those which might be given. Remember, that many of those patients were far worse than you probably are; and remember that not a few of the cases here stated as cured, had been under medical care and treatment for months or years before they applied to us.

Rheumatism is most emphatically a disease originating in the blood, and every eminent pathologist has so decided. In this disease we have acidity of the blood, and imperfect action of the liver, kidneys and skin. The secretions are retained in the system in part, and circulating in the blood, they create inflammation in the fibrous tissues of the joints, the heart and other organs. In fact, persons not unfrequently have a rheumatism of the stomach, or diaphragm, or an affection of the membranes covering the brain, without their being aware of it. Every intelligent physician knows that this disease occasionally seizes these and other organs and tissues.

Why do we specially excel in Rheumatism?

1st. Because we have made its intricate nature a special study

2d. Because we re-establish the functions of the liver, kidneys and skin.

3d. Because we have agents which act specifically upon a rheumatic diathesis, or condition of the blood.

4th. Because we have tested and proved the efficacy of our treatment of Rheumatism, and know the effects of the agents which we use in this disease, and which are peculiarly and emphatically our own.

5th. Because it is entirely original and of our own discovery—as most of our remedies are—which we use in the treatment of other diseases.

Human Decay.
General Constitutional Debility.

Every man, whether he lives in the country or city, knows that the number of debilitated persons is vastly greater than formerly. In fact there are, in almost every village in our land, persons whose only apparent disease is debility, weakness. They are generally pale, though not always; they have cold hands and feet; they are subject to chilly feelings and headache, and a languid and tiresome feeling; and not unfrequently they are dyspeptic and gloomy, and are constantly wondering why they do not get stronger. There are hundreds of such persons now, where there was one thirty years ago.

In other cases the cause of this debility is most manifest; there is an impoverished condition of the blood—a deficiency of certain chemical elements without which the blood cannot have its vitality. The person is weak and debilitated, because the blood is so impoverished as not to afford strength. It is anæmic, and the person can never have strength until the requisite blood medicines are given.

In many other cases other elements are wanting in the blood, more especially such as nourish the nervous system. People are often in this condition who have incessant business cares, and thus exhaust these chemical elements of the blood. Those whose habits are sedentary, and whose exercise is almost exclusively mental, are in this condition—such as students, teachers, editors, clergymen and others whose pursuits or circumstances render their lives full of care and anxiety. In other persons, not specially nervous nor having very constant mental care or exercise, this condition of the blood exists from another and entirely different cause. There is some exhausting disease of the kidneys, or bladder, or some other organ. Many persons suffer from great debility, prostration and mental anxiety who do not even dream the disease from which they are suffering. Many suffer from a debility of some delicate nature, concerning which they do not feel free to speak to their physician. Many middle-aged, or even young gentlemen and ladies apply to us to cure this loss of strength. It makes their lives miserable, and those of their companions and friends also. Cases of this kind have been supposed to exist mostly in the city, but we have very numerous cases of this kind applying to us every day from the country—in fact, from every section of the United States. We have brought happiness to many a man's home, by reviving his vitality, and we are daily in receipt of grateful letters of this kind from all classes of suffering humanity.

No intelligent observer has failed to discover the lurking FOE which lies hidden at the bottom of much of this human woe and deterioration of our race. Youthful indiscretions are the bane of civilized society in all countries and in all grades of life. Fathers, mothers and guardians, who have the care and training of the rising generation, should watch with vigilance this secret enemy, and, at his very first approach, despoil him of his power.

To those of either sex who have arrived at the years of discretion, a warning voice may be sufficient, coming as it does from one who has stood upon the battle-field of this inglorious destruction for thirty years, and beheld its desolations and premature deaths. It comes from one who has painfully witnessed the wreck of frail and beautiful childhood, of promising youth, and hopeful maturity upon this fatal rock. Exalted purposes and cherished ambition, and all the excellencies that make up the sum-total of useful and brilliant lives, in this and the future existence, have, in many neglected cases, been buried in the depths of oblivion, by the foolish and degrading habits to which we refer.

I will simply add, that, after an experience of thirty years, in which I have made the treatment of these diseases, very largely, a specialty, I am confident that in nine cases out of ten I can restore such to health.

My remedies are not only my own by *discovery*, but they have been tested with happy success in thousands of cases throughout the land.

Do not fear to write freely and fully all the symptoms, with age, sex, occupation, and all the essential and peculiar facts in the case, and a confidential reply may be expected by next mail.

Spinal Irritation.

Because of impurity of the blood, the humors are liable to settle upon any delicate organ or tissue. The lungs, the stomach and the uterus are the organs most often and seriously affected by bad humors. But the spinal nerve becomes affected much oftener than is generally supposed. Press directly with the thumb and fingers upon the spinal column, and some portion of it will be found to be tender, in a great majority of chronic cases; or press upon the back along the sides of the spine, one or two inches from it, and the branches of the spinal nerve will, some of them, be found very sensitive. This disease is often overlooked, and many persons are doctored for months for rheumatism, neuralgia, dyspepsia, heart disease, sciatica, womb disease, costiveness, nervousness and prostration, who are in reality not troubled with these diseases at all, but who suffer from spinal irritation. Hundreds suffer uselessly, either because this disease is not appreciated, or because those who doctor it have not the knowledge of its required remedies. Hundreds of scrofulous persons in every section of our land have this scrofulous humor settled upon the spine, and these patients become poor, nervous, wretched and wrecked invalids, confined to their beds for years. They are doctored by various doctors, for numerous diseases which they never had; or which, if they had them in a slight degree, these diseases were only the manifestations and developments of SPINAL IRRITATION.

We succeed eminently in these cases, because we "strike at the root;" we purify the blood. Another reason why we succeed is because our external remedies, which we apply by rubbing on the spine, are so effectual and valuable—different entirely from any thing ever published in any work on this much-discussed subject of medical literature, and different entirely from those that can be learned in any medical college. Persons suffering from this disease can judge of the efficacy of our remedies in these cases very soon. Only a few days will convince the most skeptical.

Diseases of Females.

In a professional pamphlet like this, designed for general reading, we cannot speak fully and freely on the several diseases to which females are subject. A few words only we will say. Every physician, as well as every experienced nurse, must have noticed how common are these diseases. Indeed, the number of really healthy adult females is comparatively few. Hundreds and thousands suffer more from general debility, want of strength, and nervous exhaustion than from any other disease. The liver and stomach, and other organs which prepare the food for blood, do not perform their duty well, and the system becomes impoverished, weak, and nervous. Liver complaint is the principal cause of this debility in a very large proportion of cases. Debility, poor blood, eruptions and discolorations of the skin, irregular appetite, and generally costiveness and headache, belong to this class of cases. We have cured thousands of them, and hence realize their frequency and become perfectly acquainted with their treatment.

We also treat very numerous cases of deficient or profuse, or too frequent or painful menstruation, and send efficient remedies daily, through every mail, to any post-office in the United States. Very numerous, also, are the cases of leucorrhea or whites, pruritus or itching, inflammation, ulcers, tumors, and prolapsus or falling and other displacements, barrenness, and other diseases, both functional and organic. These diseases, together with every variety of private disease, have occupied much of our time and attention. Without boastful parade, we wish to say that we trust we merit the large patronage bestowed upon us by the ladies of America in these diseases, by the efficiency of our cures and the confidential manner in which we have kept every professional trust. If we were to boast of any thing, it would be that no lady, married or single, has ever been deceived and betrayed to those false friends who are forever surmising and quizzing the country doctor.

Of course we can give no testimonials of our cures of these cases. It would be a breach of good faith to do so, even when patients were willing; for we claim that every case of this kind belongs only to the patient and her chosen physician. We will only add that our experience has been so large that there is no case of this kind, whether recent or of long standing, and whether common or rare in its occurrence, which we have not seen and treated.

Catarrh and Throat Disease.

This disease commences sometimes in the throat, sometimes in the passages of the nose, sometimes in the passages between the throat and internal ear (eustachian tubes), sometimes in the upper air-tubes to the lungs, and sometimes in the stomach. Whenever this disease exists there is an unhealthy condition of the lining membrane—called the mucous membrane. Sometimes this membrane is inflamed and red; sometimes it is congested and relaxed and flabby; sometimes it is covered with little grayish-white spots, called canker, or apthae; sometimes little ulcers form and heal, and then are reproduced and heal again. In many cases the catarrh will first effect one portion of the mucous membrane, and then another portion, and then return to the original seat of the disease; and thus change from place to place, changing its seat from time to time.

The nature of the disease is a weakening or degeneration of the membrane, wherever it occurs. The membrane has not a healthy condition, but one of impaired vitality, want of tone, or disease. So far as the development of the disease is concerned, this weakness, or irritation, or relaxation, may commence in the throat, or in the stomach, or in the nose; and it may, in so far, be considered a local disease. But it is not a local disease as to its *cause*. The cause is impure and irritating blood, and this irritation and weakness settles upon the *weak spot*. The membrane is weakened by its constant exposure to the varied temperatures of our climate, and its varied degrees of moisture. The membrane thus weakened becomes the seat of disease, because it is weak; for it is a general law of disease that it attacks the weakest organs or weakest point of the system. You may cure this local development of the disease a hundred times and it may do no permanent good, unless you cure also the impure condition of the blood, and strengthen the system. Any man who has had the catarrh for years knows this to be true from his own experience.

Our success in catarrh has been universally conceded. No person, so far as we know, has every attempted to deny it.

Why have we been successful?

1st. Because we purify the blood, and thus remove the cause which is so constantly reproducing the disease.

2d. Because our method of using remedies reach every portion of the diseased membrane. This is a very important point. The ordinary treatment does not reach the extensive cavities of the nose, lined by the schneiderian membrane; neither does it reach the air-tubes of the upper part of the lungs; nor does it ever reach the tubes between the throat and ears. Our directions show the patient how to apply it to every portion of these membranes.

3d. Because our experience in the use of agents has taught us the very best agents to permanently cure this disease. Hundreds of formulas for the treatment of the passages affected by catarrh have been published; but we unhesitatingly declare that nine out of every ten, professional or empirical, have done no permanent good, and many of them are highly irritating and injurious.

Our cures of catarrh have been so numerous that we scarcely know where to commence choosing our testimonials. We will present a few of those original "voices of the people;" and invite the honest scrutiny of every man of common sense, whether educated or not, to the views we have just presented.

Before introducing our evidence, in proof of our success, we must call attention to just one point. It is this: We all know that catarrh is more prevalent than almost any other disease, especially in all the middle and northern portions of the United States, and that it forms the introduction to consumption in more than two-thirds of all the cases of consumption. It is nature's warning that the blood is impure, and that this impurity is developing itself into a disease of the membrane, in the form of catarrh. Catarrh is nature's outlet for disease; for if it did not exist, the same impurities would be developed primarily upon the delicate tissues of the lungs and kidneys, and would be vastly more fatal. If you have the catarrh, remember it is a warning signal to apprise you of the impurities of the blood. Purify the blood and cure the catarrh before it is too late—before the irritation and inflammation and debility of the membrane of the throat extends to the lungs and invites the deposit of tubercles and ulceration of those organs.

Epileptic Fits.

This most horrible disease has, of late, become so very prevalent and obstinate in its character, that we feel called upon to give the people a more intelligible idea of it than is generally given by physicians for the masses.

Epilepsy is a peculiar affection of the brain and nervous system, which at certain periods results in an irregular convulsive action of the nerves, called spasms, or fits.

There are many causes that produce this dreaded affection; the most common of which are injuries of the brain or spine, or eruptions that have been driven in by improper treatment—mental or physical exhaustion, worms, impurities of the blood, irritation of the mucous membrane of the stomach and bowels. In females, any derangements of the peculiar function of their sexual organs is a prolific cause of their fits; more especially during the ages from fifteen to fifty, or during those periods of female life when the brain and nervous system are so prone to take on morbid irritation, by the operation of specific changes in the animal economy.

Functional or organic diseases of the LIVER and STOMACH are also most frequent causes of epilepsy. Improper and irregular habits of living, such as over-eating, especially food of an indigestible character. Intemperance in the use of spirits, or tobacco. These, with many other causes, conspire, directly and indirectly, to produce and prolong Epilepsy.

There is still another most fatal cause which produces, directly and indirectly, at least three-quarters of all the cases of this disease that we have to treat; and that cause will be found by reading my article in this little book, entitled "HUMAN DECAY." Parents should read it ! We have had a very large experience in the treatment of this trouble. During the past thirty years, thousands of such cases have been brought to us, and our new and specific remedies have, in a large majority of cases been successful; cures have been effected in hundreds of cases where all hope had fled and dark despair had undisputed sway. In fact there are only a few cases of Epileptic Fits met with that can be called *hopelessly* incurable.

While under treatment for this malady the patient should observe all of the laws of life and health, and make every effort to throw off and fully master the enemy by mental and physical harmony and strength. It must be remembered that the deplorable result of Epilepsy is to destroy the intellect and render its subjects imbecile, and forever IDIOTIC—a condition of life, above all others, to be feared and dreaded by every sensitive mind.

Those who are the victims of the evil alluded to above, are hereby invited to write me a full and plain statement of their cases, and I will, with the utmost candor and fairness, give my opinion of the case, with the cost of the treatment for the same, by return mail. Make an effort to retain *Reason*, *Memory* and *Self-hood*, and all that is dear to a human soul.

—

Other Diseases.

The field of labor to which we have devoted many years has been that of Chronic Diseases generally. Almost all of these arise from diseases of the liver and blood; and almost all cases of diseases of the liver and blood are connected with other local or constitutional diseases. Costiveness, Piles, Prolapsus of the Rectum, Scrofula, Tumors, Eruptions and other Skin diseases, Dropsy, Kidney Disease, Chronic Diarrhœa, Catarrh, Bronchitis, Enlarged Tonsils, Diabetes, Rheumatism and Neuralgia have largely been treated.

Persons suffering from these affections, like those before mentioned in this pamphlet, are very apt to apply to their ordinary medical counsel. Now, the time and study of the country physician are
mostly busily occupied with fevers and rheumatism, or some other kind
of acute diseases. They take his thoughts and make for him a great
daily responsibility. If he be a man of any considerable success and
acumen and an agreeable and manly address, he has usually enough
of these cases to task all his energy and take all his time. He has
neither time, taste, books nor patience to successfully investigate any
original method of treating chronic cases. Nor does he have variety
or numbers enough of them, to afford him a good test of the relative
success of different methods of treatment.

Now, we have no time to visit fever cases, or acute cases generally,
but use all our time to investigate and treat chronic cases. We
devote our whole attention to them, from day to day, and year to year.
The relative value of hundreds of plants has been thoroughly tested
in so many cases, that for every case we can at once decide upon the
remedy which will be successful.

In consequence of this course, and having largely advertised our
business, the number of rare and afflicted cases which has been presented to us has been incredible indeed. As a center of medical correspondence, our enterprise is beyond all question the most extensive
in the world. We presume that there may be many large hospitals,
both in this country and in Europe, where more patients apply for
surgical operations and surgical advice; but there is no institution in
the known world where so many persons apply for medical advice as
at our office.

What is the Evidence I shall be Cured ?

You have now read my THEORY, and the REASON WHY I am
successful. Thousands of patients who have risen from their beds of
sickness, all over the land, are sending me letters stating their recovery and gratitude. In the limits of this pamphlet I cannot present
the reader with one in a hundred. If, however, the reader should
feel the least doubt at all, let him write to any of the parties named in
the long list of testimonials and references.

TESTIMONIALS OF CURES.

Supported by Honorable Men! Read!! Read!!!

" R. LEONIDAS HAMILTON, M.D.:

"*Dear Sir:* Duty prompts me to a most grateful acknowledgment of the astonishing success of your treatment in my case. For nearly three years I had suffered from Catarrh, Nervous Rheumatism, Liver Complaint and Extreme Nervousness, insomuch that life had become an intolerable burden, and death was looked for as my only release ; physically and mentally broken down, I was utterly unable to do the duties of a minister, and was preparing to retire from the ranks when providentially my eye fell on your advertisement in the *N. Y. Methodist.* I had already traveled far and expended so much in the vain effort to secure a cure, that it was with great reluctance and little hope that I addressed you. Your reply inspired me with hope—your remedies were received and taken, and the result was as marvelous to those who knew my condition as it was gratifying to myself. In three weeks I was again in the pulpit preaching with unusual vigor, and if my services are of any value to the church, it is indebted to you, under God, for their continuance. You may refer to me at any time, and I shall be ever pleased to bear testimony to your extraordinary skill.   " Yours truly,   Rev. JOSEPH JONES,
        " Saint Joseph, Mich.

Cured after all Hopes had Fled.

"MADISONVILLE, Penn.

" Prof. R. L. HAMILTON—*Dear Sir:* Shortly after I commenced to use your remedies I felt the disease beginning to give way, and I have been improving ever since. My neighbors have often spoken of the improvement in my looks, and I know that I have not felt as well for four years as I do now. I believe you understand your business, and can do all you claim to do. Your remedies have proved, in my case, wonderful, and they wrought for me the blessed and joyous feeling of health, vigor, life, and freedom, the power to work and enjoy myself. Doctor, I thank you for your past kindness and faithful attention to me while under your care.

        " M. J. WEBSTER."

48

Dyspepsia and Constipation Cured.

Mr. S. S. Parker, of Alabama, Genesee County, N. Y., writes:

"My wife has wholly recovered since using your medicine. Previous to applying to you she was unable to take the least food or drink, except corn starch and bread coffee. Her bowels would not move for eighteen days at a time, and then forced by the most unpleasant efforts. Since the third day after taking your medicine she has taken her ordinary meals of rational food with very little inconvenience, and her bowels move regular and easy. Her feet and limbs, which previously required a jug of hot water, day and night, for a long time, to keep them warm, are now warm enough of themselves. Her nervous debility, which was past endurance, is much better, and she once more enjoys her nights in sweet sleep. She sits up all day, whereas she was only moved from one bed to another for making and change. May God bless and cause you to live long and bless with your remedies the thousands of poor invalids that are suffering for want of medical treatment."

Is Thankful!

Mrs. Abel Goodnough, of Shelburn Falls, Mass., writes:

"The medicines you sent me were received and have been taken as directed. I feel that it is but an act of justice to state, and it gives me great pleasure to do so, that I have been benefited by your valuable remedies far beyond all expectations, or the most sanguine hopes of my friends. I shall ever feel grateful to God that I was led to use the means with which he was pleased to bless me, and to you for your faithfulness in furnishing me with medicines that restored me to almost perfect health, after having suffered for years with diseases which were believed to be incurable. Indeed, I am well, and think I need no more medicine."

Most Wonderful!

Mrs. Josephine S. Hatch, Provincetown, Mass., writes:

"Prof. R. L. HAMILTON:

"*Dear Sir:* Believing a statement of my sickness and wonderful cure would be a benefit to many similarly diseased, I send you this certificate. I cannot remember the time when I was really well. Two years ago I was taken with a pain in my right side, which at times was very bad; but I was unwilling to give up and call myself sick, and the medicine I got from our family physician doing no good, I suffered in silence. In December, 1863, my side was so swollen and so painful that I could not wear my clothes. While in this condition, Mrs. Emeline Stover, of Industry, Franklin County, Me., came here on a visit, and told me how your valuable medicine had cured her of liver complaint, and she knew I had it; but I could not make up my mind to send to you then, and after a time forgot it. My side got no better, and on the 18th of May, 1864, in lifting beyond my strength, I broke the ligament in my back, and was obliged to give out entirely and go to bed. I could not turn myself in bed, and to lift me from one bed to the other, as they did once a week to make my bed, seemed as though it would take my life. I was obliged to lie on my back all the time, my head even with my body. I took my food in this position. What I suffered no one can ever know. My head ached all the time dreadfully, my side grew worse, was very painful, my back very bad; and to make matters worse, I had so much inflammation in stomach, side and bowels, that I could not take much that was strengthening. I cannot begin to tell one-half that I had to contend with, and if I could, I doubt if it would be believed. Shortly after I was taken sick I commenced to have a sort of fits, and the weaker I got the oftener I had them, and these alone, I knew, would cause my death if not soon cured. The first symptom of them would be rapid beating of the heart; next it would seem as though my heart did not beat at all, and my pulse stops, and I struggle for breath.

"These spells would sometimes last an hour, and they have often thought I was dying. My feet and hands would be cold, and have every appearance of death. I had a very good physician, but he did me no good, and I gave myself up to die. One day some friends came to see me, and brought me some things. After they were gone, I took up the paper and noticed your advertisement—read it, for want of something to do—remembered what Mrs. Stover had told me, and resolved to send. You wrote back that you could cure me permanently, if I commenced then; said my disease was of the liver and digestive organs. I had faith, and wanted your medicine. I had to talk a great deal to do away with the prejudices of many of my friends. I commenced taking your medicine on the 20th of November, and the result was glorious—far beyond my expectations. I began to gain immediately; my headache left me, I slept well, was cheerful and suffered but little. Still, I had no use of my limbs, and no one thought I ever would again. The second lot of medicine I had, you said, 'I will have you on your feet in a month, or two at the most.' I really laughed at the idea, for I then could not turn myself, move my feet, or hold my head up; but, strange as it may seem, in five weeks from that date I was so much better that they put me on my feet, and I, for the second time, LEARNED TO WALK. I have gained fast ever since. I sit up all day, walk out, and am about all day. My recovery is looked upon as little short of a miracle by hundreds who know the circumstances; and I often hear the remark, ' He must be more than a MAN who has done this.' I have had many to see me in regard to my sad condition. I thank you many times for what you have done for me, and I shall ever remember with gratitude the man who, under God, has cured me of one the most distressing diseases, the liver complaint."

"Takes Pleasure in Making Known the Good Results."

Mr. J. H. Moshell, of Columbus, Georgia, writes:

" I received your medicine and took it as directed. The effect was entirely satisfactory. Have handed out the circulars you sent me, and take great pleasure in making known the good result."

A Voice from Western New York.

Mr. John Fletcher, Sr., of Oswego, N. Y., writes:

" I am happy to inform you that the disagreeable symptoms I had when I wrote to you first have all left me, and I do not require any more medicine. I followed your advice strictly and carefully, and the result has been successful. So long as I live, so long as my memory retains its seat, so long will I retain and cherish feelings of the deepest gratitude to you ; and wherever I may be in this world, I will recommend every person I know in want of medical treatment to Professor Hamilton."

Almost Insane, but Cured !

Mrs. Cyrus Gordon, of Rushford, Alleghany Co., N. Y., writes:

" I hardly remember when I have felt as well as now. The nervous, desponding feelings are gone, and I feel more like enjoying life. Had it not been for your medicines, I believe I would still have been dragging myself around, with no energy, and entertaining gloomy, desponding thoughts. I shall do all I can to induce my female friends, of whom I have many, who are diseased as I was, to apply to you."

"Rests Well Nights."

Mr. Willis De Long, of South Edmeston, Otsego Co., New York, writes:

" I received your medicines in due time, and have used them with great benefit. Previous to taking the remedies, I could not lie on the left side, nor rest scarcely any nights. My sleep is now sound and refreshing, and I can lie on either side. All the bad feelings about my stomach and sides are gone, and I begin to feel like my former self again."

"Money Not Thrown Away."

Mr. Job Coslett, of Danville, Montour County, Penn., writes:

"I received the medicine you sent, and before I finished taking it I was able to work, and have been ever since. When I expressed my intention to try your remedies, many of my neighbors said I 'would throw away my money.' I feel that I have not thrown it away, for I received great benefit—indeed, I may say, a *perfect cure.*"

Saved from the Grave.

Mr. J. H. Jewell, of Sylvania, Pa., writes:

"I am trying to have those that are diseased send to you at once, and especially those that have the liver complaint, as I know that you are as sure to cure that every time, as the person is to take your remedies. I know that if it had not been for your remedies I should have been in my grave long before now, for I was clean gone, as you know; and if my testimony is worth any thing to you, you are at liberty to make such use of it as you may see fit, for I feel as if you had saved me from my grave."

Voice from the South.

Mrs. Lethea A. Smith, of Evergreen, Avoyelles Parish, La., writes:

"I feel and know now that I am gaining rapidly all the time, and I know not how to express my gratitude to you for relieving me of pain and misery. I have no more gloomy forebodings; menses are regular, digestion good; in short, I feel like my former self again. Any thing I can do for you, by influencing others to apply, shall be done with earnestness and great pleasure. Send me some circulars, for I feel that one should be in the hands of every diseased person throughout our impoverished Southern country."

A Case of Piles Cured.

Carrie E. Phillips, of Middletown Center, Susquehanna County, Penn., after making application for a friend of hers, adds:

"As for myself, my story is soon told. I am well again, thanks to the Lord and your medicines. I believe you have saved me from an untimely grave. You have cured me from the liver complaint and the piles. My sufferings from the latter disease (incident, I believe, to the former) were intolerable. I cannot express my thanks to you for what you have done for me, and the prompt attention and solicitude you manifested while doing it. God will be your rewarder. If I, or any other of my friends, are sick again, you will hear from us."

A Cure of Salt Rheum and Scrofula.

Miss Charlotte Rhoades, of Cortlandt Center, Kent Co., Mich., writes under recent date:

"This is the first winter in *eleven years* that my hands have not troubled me with Scrofula and Salt Rheum. It is your remedies that have accomplished this. When I see any one out of health, I tell them to at once write to you if they want to be helped."

Case of Asthma.

"AFTON, N. Y.

"To Prof. R. L. HAMILTON—*Dear Dr.:* It was between six and seven years that I was afflicted with that dire malady, the Asthma, and after employing the best medical skill in the country, and taking all the patent medicines recommended, without avail or any permanent relief, I began to think there was no cure for it; but noticing an advertisement of yours in one of the New York papers, it was with the greatest reluctance I wrote you, as I then expected it would not benefit me, and would be worse than useless. In this I was greatly disappointed, as I had not taken the medicine more than two weeks before I was able to do light work on the farm. Before this, I could not attend to any business, being completely prostrated, and after taking two packages, considered myself perfectly cured, and my health fully established, the bronchial difficulties and all bad symptoms being entirely removed. All this is attributable to your unrivaled medicine, under the Divine sanction, which, I trust, with me, will ever be remembered with gratitude. I cannot close this communication without an expression of my heartfelt gratitude and thanks for the timely aid you rendered my daughter in Consumption. The efficiency of the medicine in her case has been truly miraculous. That hectic cough and flush on her cheek, with the other consumptive symptoms, have entirely left her, and now. after a period of five months, she is enjoying good health and is quite robust, so much that she has engaged to teach school this Summer. You are at liberty to show this letter to any similarly afflicted, or publish it, as you think proper. Any letter of inquiry I will cheerfully answer. I am, dear Doctor, with many thanks, your humble servant, JOSEPH LITTLE."

Read, Ye Afflicted !

Mrs. Samuel A. Firman, of Carversville, Penn., writes:

"My daughter now enjoys better health than she has had before in many years. She seems to be perfectly well. Your medicine has cured her."

Good Report from Indiana !

"PLYMOUTH, Marshall Co., Ind.

" Prof. R. L. HAMILTON :

"*Dear Doctor :* Through the helping hand of an all-wise God, I consider you my life and health preserver. Were it not for the medical treatment received from you, I feel assured that I would have been in my grave. I think it has been about two years since I have taken any medicine, and my health has been better since I used your remedies than it has ever been before in over ten years. The bleeding at the lungs, and the long train of other complaints, of which you cured me, were pretty good tests of your skill and treatment, which proved to be a success. My friends were greatly surprised at my speedy recovery, and the doctors had to give it up, and acknowledge that there was no 'humbug' in the case. Every one about here who has tried your remedies has been greatly benefited by them. and I can most cheerfully recommend them to all persons who are afflicted with disease. A friend of mine has informed me that your medicine was of more benefit to him than all he had ever taken. Hoping that you may live long to heal the afflicted and suffering, and knowing that you will ever have my well wishes and esteem, I am, with much respect,   JAMES C. TUTTLE."

A Sad Case, Surely !

The following needs no comment :

"NORTH EGREMONT, Berkshire Co., Mass.

" DR. HAMILTON :

"*Dear Sir :* I was troubled for some years with liver complaint and bilious colic, which at times was so severe that I longed for death to end my misery. Last September I was taken down so low that my friends thought there was no help for me, and said I must die. My suffering was more than I can tell. I employed one physician after another, without experiencing any permanent relief. At last, reading of your wonderful cures in the *Independent,* I concluded to write to you, stating my case as correctly as possible, and received your answer, that you could *cure me.* I therefore ordered the medicine (my friends still doubting), which was taken as directed, and after taking it two or three days, I began to gain, and now feel quite *well,* having worked at my trade (carpenter and joiner) for some weeks past. I confidently recommend all afflicted as I was to place themselves under your treatment, for I am convinced you understand your business and can do what you claim.

"Yours truly,   CHAS. POTTER."

Interesting Case!

SOUTH WOODSTOCK, Conn.

Mrs. L. H. Palmer gives a history of her case, which, as she says, "was so remarkable that strangers came many miles to see me, the same as they would a great curiosity. I seem," she writes, "to have all the complaints a person can have and live—indeed, I seem to live but to suffer. I have headache, sore throat, with a general disorganization of the system; am touched with a dry, tight cough, short breath, very costive; have night sweats, and at times afflicted with the piles, which are intolerably painful. Now I suffer with the cold, and again seem burning with the heat. I have not had a menstrual discharge for fifteen weeks; I have sharp, running pains in my hips and kidneys, and my liver is apparently torpid and inactive."

The medicines needed by Mrs. P. were at once forwarded, and the benefits derived from them are apparent from the following extract from one of her substantial letters:

"Although I had begun to be encouraged by the slight improvement, yet I felt that a crisis was coming—one which I dared not to contemplate. You can imagine my agreeable surprise when I passed the critical period with less pain than I ever felt in my life. From that time I began to improve rapidly; nature seemed to have been aroused under the magical influence of your remedies; my strength returned; my mind appeared to be relieved of all melancholy, and again the pathway of life opened brightly before me. Only last week I returned to my native place, from whence I was taken years ago on my bed, hardly expected by my friends to reach my journey's end alive. When my old acquaintances saw me returning comparatively well, they could hardly believe that such a miracle could be wrought by medicine; they say it seems 'like one raised from the dead,' to see me moving around again. As long as I live I shall be a walking advertisement of your truly wonderful healing powers. Words cannot speak my gratitude. Once more I find happiness in living. If ever I succeed in accomplishing any good, I shall attribute it all to you."

When Doctor's Disagree Who Shall Decide?

Miss Mary C. Webster, of Pilcher, Belmont Co., Ohio, writes:

"When I first told my regular physician who had been attending me that I was taking your remedies, he said: 'I tell you, Miss Webster, there is no use in taking Dr. Hamilton's or any other doctor's medicine, for you have no constitution on which to build; there is not sufficient vitality in your system to respond to the action of the medicine; no power on earth can save you, and if you live a month 'twill be owing to the favorable condition of the weather.' The fact that I am still living, and far better than three years ago, is evidence that the doctor was not very correct in his remedies. I feel that it is your remedies alone that have kept me out of my grave. I attribute all I enjoy to the favor of God and your treatment; and shall ever feel grateful for my deliverance from what seemed an untimely death."

Important Correspondence.

By permission, I publish below the substance of a correspondence between a well-known clergyman of this city and one of Chicago, Ill., in relation to myself and my successful treatment of diseases. It explains itself:

"To the Rev. J. T. M., Chicago, Ill.—*Dear Sir:* You write me to inquire about Dr. R. L. Hamilton. I have had extensive business dealings with him; have known him as an honored member of society; have received medical advice at his hands, when suddenly stricken down by the dreadful visitation of Coup de Soleil, and have known him socially and as a friend. Dr. Hamilton possesses one of those natures gifted with a discriminating benevolence, an aptness in the selection of companionship, great versatility of business capacity, a high and exceedingly keen-sense of honor, a ready humor, a judicious reserve when among rivals in his profession, a kindness of demeanor, wholly Christian, toward those who see fit to differ from him, a noble generosity toward a fallen adversary, a keen perception of the right in any controversy, and a gentleness mixed with dignity in his carriage, which marks him as a man above all mean and low tastes. It is true that Dr. Hamilton is an eclectic in his profession of medicine. This, of course, exposes him to all the batteries of the bigots and the partisans of the pathies, if we may coin a word. He could never be sectarian in religion, he can no more belong to a water-cure school, a pill-worshiping sect, a phlebotomy-loving class, a school of sugar-pellet devotees, or expect to cure every disease by vomiting a man down to his boots with lobelia. Dr. Hamilton is simply a man of good common sense, who knows that there is good in all things medical. The leaves of the tree were given for the healing of the nations, and yet there are mineral things, and things animal, and best of all, the pure air of heaven, and the glorious sun, and the ever-flowing waters, that come in their time and place to restore the sufferer. He is most thoroughly acquainted with all the good things of all the schools. Hence, Dr. Hamilton has risen to be a marvel to the narrow-minded of all the pathics. We need not tell you, our friend, and the friend of unity in the church, how glad we are to introduce to you the beloved physician of our acquaintance. We who mourn the schism in the Church of Christ, can appreciate a man who, by a judicious eclecticism, seeks to unite the sad and often terrific sectarianism of the doctors.

"Dr. Hamilton is, therefore, a specific rather than a patent medicine doctor. He has a greater faculty of versatility, and can do more things, and do them well, than any man I ever met. As a business man, he could rival Stewart, had he the heart, or rather the no-heart, to worship Mammon. We most cheerfully commend him to your confidence. He will counsel you wisely in the terrible battles you may have with acute or chronic diseases.

"Yours cordially,

"Rev. H. D. KIMBALL, New York City."

A Case of Diarrhea of Two Years' Standing Cured.

Mr. Ira D. Allen, Postmaster at Pole Grove, Wisconsin, writes:

"Your medicines I have received, and used as directed. Most of the time for two years previous to applying to you, I had suffered severely with diarrhea, and had tried most every remedy, but to no purpose. I have strong reasons to believe that your remedies will have the desired effect, as I am gaining finely."

Hope On, Hope Ever.

"HUDSON, Ill.

"*Dear Doctor:* I delayed writing to you that I might see whether the relief I had realized from your valuable medicines would be as lasting and permanent as it was unexpected and magical. I am glad to be able to say that I have experienced no relapse, and I feel it due to the sick and afflicted, and your indefatigable labors in their behalf, that I should acknowledge your skill and success in the treatment of Liver Disease.

"Having suffered three years from a very disordered and deranged state of the liver, and having tried the best physicians in Jacksonville, Ill., an adjoining town, and receiving no benefit, I determined to try your remedies, of which I had frequently read, and passed them by as a humbug. I tried one course, was much relieved; tried another, and felt so much relieved as almost to forget my former troubles. Since that time I have continued to convalesce, and am now, comparatively speaking, a new man. I shall never forget my indebtedness to you, nor forget to cherish the remembrance of your name. "Truly yours,
"ARTHUR W. HARVEY."

Case of an Aggravated Stomach Difficulty.

Mrs. Mary A. Whitford, of East Florence, N. Y., writes:

"Prof. HAMILTON—*My Dear Sir:* Your medicines were all promptly received, and taken according to directions. Louise is a well girl again. I never expected to see her so well as she is. She can do a good day's work, and can walk a mile to Sabbath-school and meeting. She sends her most sincere thanks, and says you have done a 'great thing' for her. You have restored her sinking health in a very short time. We shall be grateful to you so long as we live."

A Clergyman's Evidence.

"Boonton, N. J.

"R. L. Hamilton, M.D.:

"*Dear Sir:* It is with pleasure I communicate the result of the use of your medicines. When I first visited your office in New York, I could scarcely walk from the cars before your door into the office without exhaustion. With all your prestige as a successful physician, I had but little hope that you could cure me. There was nothing strange in this. Four years and four months had passed away, but during that period I had suffered constantly with chronic diarrhea and piles. I had some of the best physicians, and used every thing I heard of that I could procure, but all in vain. Why should I think that you could do me more good than others? But, sir, justice and gratitude compel me to say that after the use of your medicine for a few months the result was a complete cure. I ceased the use of your medicine about the 1st of September, and had no return of diarrhea until the 15th of January, 1864, and that attack I could trace to its cause; indeed, sir, I cannot expect to be freed from liabilities to attacks of disease any more than other men. I wish I had the voice of seven thunders, and could assemble all the sick in the world, I would direct them to you, sir, as one fully competent to heal, and whose generous and noble nature would not allow of exorbitant charges.

"Yours, truly,   Rev. GEO. H. JONES."

A Celebrated Physician Acknowledges Beat.

"Watkon, Allemakee Co., Iowa.

"Dear Doctor: I feel that it would be injustice to you, as well as to myself, not to acknowledge what you have done for me. Last year I was sick, attended by two said-to-be good physicians, and given up to die. A neighbor of mine wrote to you for me, stating my disease, and you answered you could and would cure me. Your medicines were received, and after taking them till I was able to sit up to have my bed made, my family doctor called, and, seeing how fast I was gaining, said that it was not your remedies that were benefiting me so much, but his, and made me believe it. I stopped taking yours, and continued taking his, until I realized it was killing me, and then commenced taking yours again, and soon recovered, and have been well ever since. I am able to perform the most arduous manual labor, which I have not done in 16 years. My family physician (the one who doctored me) said the other day: 'Mr. Beeman, had it not been for Prof. Hamilton, you would have died last Summer, in spite of all we could do.' I submit the case of my wife for your consideration, with every confidence that you will do as well by her as you have done by me. Believe me ever gratefully and truly yours,

"CYRUS BEEMAN."

Liver Disease of Ten Years' Standing Cured.

Mr. George W. Crocker, of South Valley, Otsego County, N. Y., writes:

"I have used a portion of the medicines prepared for me, and am much gratified in informing you that I have gained twenty per cent. in health. It is surprising to me, as I had not seen a well day for ten years previous to applying to you. I consider your remedies truly wonderful."

UNPARALLELED SUCCESS !

Gov. Jacobs, of Kentucky.

His Excellency, Ex-Lieut-Gov. R. T. Jacobs, writes us from Westport, Ky., as follows:

"Dr. R. L. Hamilton—*My Dear Sir:* I feel desirous of testifying to you my profound gratitude for the great medical skill with which you have treated me, and by which, under the blessing of Divine Providence, I have been completely restored to health. Since 1865, I have been subject to terrible and most alarming attacks. During that time my whole system seemed to be out of order. My blood was sluggish and concentrated to my head. My face would be flushed, while the lower extremities were as cold as ice apparently, and gave me constant pain. The top of my head would often feel as if I had an immense weight grinding and crushing in the skull, and this would generally end in congestion of the brain, when my life, for a time, would be despaired of. I never knew what it was to be free from a headache or severe pain beneath the eyes and running around to the back of the head and spine. My liver was so torpid that unless constantly under the influence of Calomel I would be seized with congestion of the brain. My stomach was very much out of order, and my tongue heavily coated. My kidneys would pain me so that I have frequently awakened in the night in the most terrible agony. My lower extremities were nearly paralyzed, and my sides much swollen. I was all this time, at the advice of my physicians, taking Calomel, Blue Mass, Dover's Powders, with Ipecacuanha in pills, Iron and Quinine mixed, and Iron and Quinine separate, still I felt myself inevitably growing worse, and it was only a question of time, and that a very short period, too, when one of these attacks would end my earthly career. I saw your advertisement, and read it carefully, and though struck with its good sense, yet under that education which has taught us to be prejudiced against advertising physicians, I passed it by Last September I saw your advertisement again. I then determined to try your remedies, for I felt that I was fast sinking into the grave, with all that the Allopathic School could do for me.

"Death seemed inevitable. I wrote you giving my symptoms, and received promptly medicines and the assurance that you could cure me. I have taken your remedies according to directions, and I now feel entirely well. My blood circulates freely; my stomach is strong; my liver is no longer torpid; my kidneys have ceased to pain me; and now I do not know what it is to have the headache or congestion. Neither do I feel my limbs cold and paralyzed. I can cheerfully say that I enjoy an energy and life that I have not felt for years, if I ever did.

"Certainly, sir, I have abundant occasion to feel grateful to you for the great benefits received at your hands in so short a time. Suppose I do not know what your remedies are, as some urge, it is impossible for them to be as deleterious as Mercury, which rots the very life out of one, or Quinine and other such horrid stuffs, which leave the system in a worse state than they find it. I know that your medicines are of an entirely different character, from their effect upon me. They are exceedingly mild, and never gripe or sicken. I have noticed one peculiarity in your practice, and that is, you brace and build up the whole system at the same time. You not only cure the torpidity of the liver, but you strengthen the lungs and stomach, and purify the blood, thus completely restoring the whole body. If this should come under the observation of any poor sick wretch racked with pain, who finds no relief from Calomel, Quinine, Iron, and such like medicines, I earnestly appeal to him to try your most valuable discoveries, while I sincerely pray that the same wonderful results which have attended your practice with me, may result to him."

Liver and Digestive Organs Cured.

"WEEDSPORT, N. Y.

"Prof. HAMILTON.

Dear Sir : I have used three-quarters of the package of medicine you sent me, and thanks to that wise Providence, whom all should bless, for the great good they have done me. I truly believe that my disease was of the liver and digestive organs; and had I not received timely aid from your treatment, my difficulties would have terminated in liver complaint, and that I should have been incurable. I had been failing fast for the last five months previous to applying to you, although under medical treatment of three of the most skillful physicians in one of the cities of this State. Many persons are daily visiting me to see and hear of your miraculous skill, remarking that 'Prof. Hamilton must be possessed of more than a doctor's power to cure you.' Some look at me with great amazement, after noticing the great change that has taken place in my condition and appearance in so short a time. I ride or walk every day, and can walk a mile.   Truly, yours,

"Mrs. D. C. HOWE."

A Bad Case of Liver Disease Cured.

Mr. Samuel Curtis, Dacotah City, Nebraska, writes:

"Prof. R. L. HAMILTON—*Dear Sir:* Your medicines were received in due time, and I must, in justice to you, say that they worked to a charm in my complaint. I pronounce myself well. I have done more hard work in the last eight months than I ever expected to do. I cannot say too much in your praise for your skillful treatment of chronic diseases."

Chronic Diarrhea Cured.

Rev. Augustus Alvord, of Ridgebury, Conn., writes:

"Doctor HAMILTON—*Dear Sir:* When I began taking your medicines I felt almost discouraged, for my difficulty, chronic diarrhea, was of three years and a half standing, and I had consulted many physicians and had received no benefit. In a very few days after commencing to take your remedies I began to feel much better. I have not taken any medicine now for three months, and I consider myself well. I feel it a duty, as well as a pleasure, to make this statement, and I desire also to thank you for your kind attention and Christian advice."

Is Very Thankful.

Mrs. Amos Southwick, of Chester, N. H., writes:

"I cannot find language to express my grateful thanks to you, and to a kind Providence for his blessings on your individual remedies. They have truly acted like magic on my system in removing ills to which I have been subject for many years. My friends and neighbors begin to see and tell me how much better I look, I call my health good now. It has not been so good for more than thirty years. My appetite is good, and every thing I eat sets well. Nothing seems to disagree. I think you will have patients from this vicinity soon, as I am recommending your treatment to the afflicted, and they know how I have improved. I feel like another person. The pressure and rush of blood to my head, the soreness and pain in my right side and shoulder, and the swelling and bloat, are all gone. I really did not believe it possible that I could be cured of so many ills in so short a time. Long may you live, and great success may you always have in relieving the afflicted, and may Heaven's choicest blessings ever rest upon you."

Liver Disease Cured !

Read this testimony from Miss Crouch, of Schoharie County, N. Y. :

"WEST CONESVILLE.

" Dr. HAMILTON—*Respected Sir :* I embrace the present moment to write a few lines to you to inform you of the effect of some medicines received from you last spring. The medicines were prepared as soon as received, and I commenced to use them. For the first two or three days I felt very little effect. I was in this condition seven or eight days, when I discovered a change for the better was slowly taking place ; the dull, heavy headache was gone ; my sleep was quiet and refreshing ; food seemed to nourish instead of distressing me ; indeed, the best way I can express the change is this : It was like taking down an old building, repairing the waste places, and building up anew. We have delayed writing to see whether the cure was permanent or not. I have reason to believe it is lasting. I believe your remedies to be very efficacious in eradicating diseases from the system, and can with confidence recommend them to the afflicted.

" May you long be spared to bless the human family in the exercise of your great skill is the sincere wish of your very grateful friend,

"MARTHA CROUCH."

Consumption Cured.

D. Loucks, of West Martinsburg, N. Y., writes :

" R. L. HAMILTON, M.D.—*Dear Sir :* With thankfulness to a kind Providence and your skill, my daughter, Mrs. Vanderburgh, has about recovered her former good health. Our doctor says her lungs are healed. She is decidedly smart, and her countenance has much of her former healthful look. She is also improving in strength every day. My son, H. H. Loucks, is also improving. His case seems more obstinate, but is giving way. I think both of them would have been in their graves by this time, if it had not been for your treatment ; and I can assure you that I feel very thankful for your skillful and successful treatment."

" Benefited Her More than all the Remedies."

Mrs. E. A. Ellsworth, of Dannemora, Clinton Co., N. Y., writes :

" About one year ago I sent for and received your medicine, which benefited me more than all the remedies I ever used in my life, and I now want you to let me know what you can do for a neighbor of mine."

Important Cure of Liver Disease.

"Litchfield, Conn.

"Doctor Hamilton—*Dear Sir*. I took your medicines according to directions, and I feel that they have done for me what medicines never did before. I feel real well—better than I have before for five or six years, and I *know* it is what you have done for me, and I am very grateful to you for what you have done.

"ours respectfully,
"GEO. H. TROWBRIDGE."

Reports the Good Results.

"Groton, Caledonia Co., Vt.

"Dr. Hamilton—*Dear Sir:* Having about a year ago been myself completely restored to health by your wonderful medicines, after suffering with diseased liver, and believing that you saved my life, and being now in the enjoyment of better health from the result of your remedies than I have been in many years, I now write you for my sister, who has been in very poor health for the last two years. I have no doubt but that you will cure her. I herein send you a statement of her complaints, which please examine and then reply.

"I am, and ever will be truly grateful, and may Heaven reward you. EMILY A. ORR."

He Rejoices.

"Woodstock, Vt.

"Prof. R. L. Hamilton—*Dear Sir:* Previous to the receipt of your medicines, which reached me about two months ago, I had been suffering with a diseased liver of over ten years' standing. During the time, I was subject to severe headache, heartburn, sour stomach, unsteady appetite, pains in my side, and low spirits, could not rest nights, was easily excited and dull. I commenced taking your remedies, having but little faith that they would help me. It was but a few days afterward that I discovered a great and decided change in my feelings. I have gained rapidly, those bad feelings have disappeared, and I feel to-day like a new man. You have my most sincere thanks for your kindness and attention, and I advise all who are suffering from disease to apply at once to you for relief. May God's choicest blessings rest upon you through life.

"Very respectfully,
"C. A. WOODBURY."

General Consumption.

Mrs. John Sparks, of West Union, Ohio, writes:

"*Dear Doctor:* I have taken your medicines according to directions, and I am astonished at the wonderful cure they have performed in my case. I do as much work now as I ever did. I have a good appetite and sleep well, and have gained about twenty pounds. When I applied to you, our physician, and all who knew me, said I was foolish, and throwing away money, for I never could be cured. But now they talk quite differently, as they have the evidence of your skill and valuable remedies in my restoration."

Good from Iowa.

"NEW VIRGINIA, Warsaw County, Iowa.

"Prof. R. L. HAMILTON—*Dear Doctor:* I commenced taking your medicine last Spring, and feel that it has cured me. I was the most distressed looking being you ever saw when I applied to you for treatment. I was as yellow as a pumpkin; had pains in my head, breast, back, side, and shoulders, with soreness in the bowels. Nothing that I ate agreed with me. I had constant diarrhea, and my limbs seemed almost lifeless. I was gradually sinking. The doctors, and every one else who saw me, gave me up to die. But, through the kind mercy of Almighty God, and your medicine, I have been restored to health.

"Your remedies relieved me in three days after I commenced taking them, and I continued to improve rapidly until cured. Were it not for them I think I would have been, long ere this, in my grave.

"I cannot sufficiently express my thankfulness to you for the great and lasting benefit I have received by the use of your remedies.

"Yours, with respect,
"Mrs. NATHANIEL HYLTON."

The Work Goes Bravely On! Another Clergyman Cured!!

The eminent divine, Rev. J. W. Hinkley, of Athens, Maine, writes:

"My health has so far improved from the effects of your treatment that I am able to resume my pastorship. Had it not been for your medicine I should not have been living now. To you, with God's blessing, do I owe my worldly existence. I am a living exponent of the worth of your matchless remedies, and I shall hereafter deem it a part of my religious duty, to recommend all suffering with diseases of the liver or lungs to speedily apply to you. May God's blessing attend your worthy efforts for the relief of diseased and suffering humanity."

Mercifully Saves the Afflicted.

Mr. John Lewis, of Ten Mile P. O., Washington County, Penn., writes:

"The medicine you sent me last spring acted like a charm. It relieved me very soon of a deranged state of the liver, stomach, and bowels. The marked peculiarity of your remedies is, while they act directly and thoroughly on the diseased organs, they do not depress or debilitate the system, like other liver remedies I have used. I consider you fully master of your profession, and from your open, fair way of dealing with me, I deem you an upright, conscientious man, as well as an accomplished physician."

Speedily Restored.

"PEORIA, Ill.

"Prof. R. L. HAMILTON, M.D.—*Dear Sir:* The medicines which you sent me reached me in due time, and I now take pleasure in speaking of their valuable character. There is no medicine within my knowledge that equals them. I am *radically cured* of my disease, although I have not taken but little more than one-half of the quantity you sent me. Truly, you are a public benefactor, and I, therefore, cheerfully add my approbation of your medicines to the many indorsements which you have received.

"Very respectfully,
"THOMAS CONAGHAN."

Many Kind Thanks!

"AUBURN FOUR CORNERS, Susquehanna County, Penn.

"Prof. HAMILTON: I now improve the present opportunity to inform you of the result of your medicine. It has effected a permanent cure, as the agonizing pain in my right side, which has troubled me for three years, has entirely subsided. My appetite is decidedly better, and the various symptoms, which I had at the time of applying to you, have all disappeared. My health never was better than at the present time, and I attribute all to the use of your valuable medicine, for which I shall always feel very grateful, and will do all I can to induce my diseased friends and acquaintances to apply to you, for I believe your remedies to be all and every thing you claim for them. If I ever need any more medicine, or any of my family, I shall apply to you at once, as I believe it to be the surest, safest, and best to be had. I remain, yours at command,

"Mrs. S. W. SMITH."

Has Reason to be Thankful.

Mrs. Emeline Stover, of Industry, Franklin County, Maine, writes:
"I had given up the hope of ever being well, before I received your medicine. I have been well nigh cured, and attribute all—yes, *all*—to your great healing power. I have not had a symptom of that dreadful headache in over three months. Have I not reason to be thankful for the good I have received at your hands?"

Rheumatism.

JAMES D. PEASE, Esq., Trumansburg, N. Y.

"We (my wife and I) are recommending you to our acquaintances, who know what you have done for us, for they can see for themselves. Several, afflicted as my wife was (Chronic Rheumatism), will send to you, because they would have to pay twice the amount to doctors here for visits, and have besides to buy all the medicines at the drug stores. I want you to publish this as a great cure of that awful disease, Rheumatism.

It is with much satisfaction that I invite particular attention to the following voluntary statement of the eminent Divine and Missionary, the Rev. A. A. Constantine, recently located in the interior of Africa:

"No. 43 ANN STREET, New York City.

"Dr. R. LEONIDAS HAMILTON, 546 Broadway:

"*My Dear Benefactor:* A sense of duty impels me to say that your medicines have done for me what no other physician has been able to do. I have been a sufferer for many years from disease contracted while laboring as Missionary in Africa. Last fall I was declining fast, and had all the symptoms of quick consumption. I applied to you for help. You remarked, 'Before I get through with you I will make you feel several years younger than you have felt since you left Africa.' I thought but little of that, as I had often received similar assurances from eminent physicians both here and in Europe; but in less than two weeks all my symptoms were entirely changed, and my health and strength improved very fast. In a few weeks I found myself in the enjoyment of better health, and able to perform more labor, mental and physical, than at any previous time since I left Africa. May God bless you in all your researches in His great laboratory, and make you His agent in restoring thousands to health.
"Rev. A. A. CONSTANTINE."

An Old Lung Difficulty.

C. A. Smith, Esq., of Paducah, Ky., writes:

"Dear Doctor: My brother commenced taking your medicines about 11 days ago, since which time he has materially progressed toward better health. He sleeps and breathes much easier, and his strength is returning very fast. He is gaining in flesh also. He coughs much less; indeed, yesterday, he walked with me some three miles, slowly, of course, and he coughed but once during the ramble, which would not have been done at any time before for two years. You will hear from this place, in the way of other patients."

A Complicated Case.

Mrs. John D. Parmenter, of Hammond Creek, Tioga County, Pa., writes:

"Language is inadequate to express in a fitting manner, my deep and most heartfelt gratitude to you for having restored me to health by your medicines, (which I took from time to time as directed), after I had been severely afflicted for many years with a general debility of the whole nervous system, liver complaint, indigestion, and all their attendant consequences; I was much of the time unable to be about my house, but I feel that I am now well and in a condition to attend to all my domestic duties.

I am so thankful to you for the great benefits derived from your treatment, that I cannot speak too highly in your praise. I rest as well, and sleep as good nights as I ever did, and every one who knows me is greatly astonished to find my health so greatly improved, and say that they, too, must try your remedies."

Chronic Dysentery Cured.

Mr. J. N. Barnett, of Shabonier, Ill., writes:

"I received your medicines in due time, and began taking them according to directions. I was at that time in a very low state of health, and was reduced to one hundred and nineteen pounds, and was barely able to walk across my room. My stomach was so much affected that the lightest food caused me great pain, and I had diarrhœa all the time, and when I received the medicines I was afflicted also with the dysentery very badly. But after taking the medicines twelve hours I found great relief. The dysentery was cured in two or three days, and from that time on I began to mend. I gained ten pounds in eleven days, and strength in proportion; and up to this time I have gained twenty-one pounds, being heavier than I ever was before at this time of the year."

A Truly Wonderful Cure.

"DENMARK, Oxford County, Me.

"MY DEAR SIR: Believing a statement of my case would be a benefit to the public, or more especially to a person similarly diseased, I send you this certificate. One year ago last June, I was taken with a very severe pain in my right side; it continued to grow worse until I was obliged to stop all kinds of business, and finally took to my bed the most of the time. The pain was so bad that I could get no rest night or day. I suffered beyond all description; I had the advice and counsel of the best physicians in the State, and they could do me no good; all they gave me was blue pills and morphine. I continued to grow worse until about the middle of August, when I had an abscess break out on my liver; it discharged through the lungs, some pint and a half, or more, the first twenty-four hours, and then every twenty-four hours until December following, it discharged from half to one pint, and then commenced to fill up again for two weeks, when it broke again, and continued to do so every two weeks all winter, till the middle of February, when they would rise and break every few days. It seems to me I raised a barrel of thick matter, or pus; it was about the color of blood—perhaps not quite as red. It reduced me so I was a complete skeleton; the doctors all told me I must die, and that soon; they gave me nothing but morphine to ease the pain; they said I could not live more than two weeks at most; I couldn't sit up at all—not long enough to have my bed made. I coughed and raised more than any person in a consumption; I tried all the patent medicines of the day, and everything that could be thought of, and grew worse all the time. My side was so sore (outside) I couldn't bear my clothes to touch it: and to sum it all up, I was in a very bad fix, any way. A friend of mine got one of your papers, and brought it to me to look at; I read some of it, and thought I would try you—I could but die any way; I had but little hope, there was so much humbug in the world. I wrote you, I think, in March; your answer was you could cure me, and sent me some medicine. I commenced taking it the last of April. I commenced getting better from the first dose, and continued to till I was quite well. The sore never stopped discharging to fill up until after I commenced taking your medicine, and the discharge grew less every day until completely healed up, which was some time in August, since which time my health never was better. I can do as good a day's work as any other man, and stand it as well; and I do know it was your medicine that cured me, and I do sincerely and honestly believe that any person that is sick (and their case is curable), that will get your medicine and follow your directions, they will surely get cured. My advice is, friends all, if you are sick send to Prof. R. L. Hamilton, and he will cure you.

"I remain, yours forever, God bless you,

"J. B. WATSON."

Catarrh and Incipient Consumption.

Mrs. Abigail Beeman, of Waukon, Allamakee County, Iowa, says:

"I have taken your medicines as directed, and cannot express my gratitude. I had not been able to do my work for eleven years, and during that time had taken medicines from the most eminent physicians in the West, but was constantly growing worse, and was not able to sit up an hour. I fear, had it not been for your valuable medicines, I should have been in my grave. Now I sit up all day, and I am able to work."

Another Important Cure.

"MILLEN'S BAY, N. Y.

"Prof. HAMILTON—*Dear Doctor:* Rest assured that your medicine has done more for father than we ever expected could be done for him. When, some time ago, we sent to you for medicine, we expected before this to have consigned him to the silent grave; but thanks be to a merciful Providence and your valuable remedies, we are permitted to see him enjoying a good degree of health.

"M. A. FARR."

Consumption can be Cured.

Wm. Neighbors, of Omaha, Putnam County, Mo., writes:

"I take pleasure in giving you the following account of the effects of your medicines in my case. I had been confined to my house and bed for twelve months with a lingering disease. My digestive organs were in an inactive condition, my lungs were weak, and other symptoms of consumption becoming alarming, I wrote to you and gave you a statement of my case on the last of August, and received a package of medicines on September 29, and commenced taking it immediately. At that time I was so weak, short of breath, and stiff in my joints, that I could scarcely walk. After taking your medicine about five days I began to mend, and shortly after went to work, and have worked every day since."

Chronic Diarrhea Cured.

Mr. C. E. Peabody, of Groton Junction, Mass., writes:

"*Dear Doctor:* I suffered intensely with chronic diarrhea for a year, so much so that I was unable to do any business, and could not get any relief from the various medicines that the doctors ordered for me, or from the many remedies that filled the papers, until I was induced to try your medicines, which gave me instant relief, and in a short time cured me."

Liver and Lungs Badly Diseased.

"WEBSTER CITY, Iowa.

"Dr. HAMILTON—*Dear Friend :* I feel that it is due to you, as well as to all those who are afflicted with disease, to express my gratitude to you for the great benefit which I have received from the use of your medicines. For many months I had had a pain in my shoulders and side, soreness across the chest, difficulty of breathing, hacking cough, sore throat, ringing and roaring in my ears. I was very nervous and my slumbers were disturbed by frightful dreams, and it would seem almost incredible if I were to attempt to describe the objects which seemed to be before me when wide awake. Sleep was no rest to me. I had no ambition, and I had about come to the conclusion that unless I soon got relief my earthly career would soon be ended. I kept growing worse until I was confined to my bed all the time. My husband induced me to write to you, and your remedies came duly to hand, and in a very short time I began to recover, and am now ccmparatively well. I thank you, doctor, for your faithful attention, and I shall always recommend you to the afflicted.

"With much respect,

"MARY E. LYON."

Diarrhea and Liver Complaint.

"MASON CENTER, N. H.

"Doctor HAMILTON—*Dear Sir :* I feel that it is due to you, as well as all persons afflicted with chronic diseases, that I express my gratitude to you for the great benefit that I have received from your medicines. When I was taken with diarrhea, I tried the remedies used in such cases, to no purpose, and almost every one thought I must die. I was also troubled with liver complaint, so that I could not lie down with any ease. But through the helping hand of an All-Wise God, I was restored, and gratefully do I regard you as the preserver of my life and health.

"LUKE NEWELL."

Epileptic Fits Again ! Another Perfect Cure ! !

"Dr. R. L. HAMILTON—*Dear Sir :* My son was afflicted with fits for fifteen years. I read of you, and was so impressed with your new and simple theory of disease, that I would have him try your remedies. As you know, I sent for your remedies, which, with the help of God, have cured him. Words cannot express my gratitude and joy, and I wish to make it known, as I deem it a duty to all afflicted with this awful malady to do all in my power to make known to mankind the true physician. And if any doubt this you may refer them to me, and I will satisfy them that all is true. I remain yours at command,

"Mrs. EUNICE C. DOW.

"CHICOPEE, Mass., P. O. Box 96."

Asthma Cured.

Mrs. A. D. Clark, of West Waterville, Maine, writes:

"Prof. R. L. HAMILTON—*Sir:* After testing your most excellent medicines, and feeling sure that my life would not have been spared until the present time had I not used them, I feel that I could sound your fame all over the land, to all suffering humanity. When I first learned about your medicines, I was troubled with the liver complaint and the asthma, in their worst forms, and I was afflicted with other complaints, too numerous to mention. I now feel entirely changed, and have not had a symptom of the asthma for a long time."

A Clergyman's Evidence.

"POINTVILLE, N. J.

"Prof R. L. HAMILTON—*Dear Sir:* I have purposely delayed writing in order to give you the results of your remedies. The medicines came to hand in due time, and I commenced using them as instructed, and have persevered. For the first week I could not see much change; the second week there seemed to be a giving way of the disease; and at the end of the third week a decided change for the better was manifest. I am now able to walk about with ease and comfort. I send you my sincere and many thanks, and pray that God may bless and preserve your life for many years. I feel that, under the blessing of Divine Providence, you have done great things for me.   Yours, truly,

"Rev. ISAAC HUGG."

Epileptic Fits! A Splendid Cure!!

"GUILDERLAND, N. Y.

"Professor R. LEONIDAS HAMILTON—*Dear Doctor:* I now write you concerning my Epileptic Fits, of which your medicines have permanently cured me, and I send my grateful thanks, and can't but recognize you as an instrument of Divine Power in rescuing me from a terrible death. Words cannot express my gratitude and joy, and I wish to make it known far and near, as I deem it a solemn duty, to all afflicted with this awful malady, to do all in my power to make known to mankind the true physician. And if any doubt the authenticity of this, you may refer them to me, and I will satisfy them that all is true, and I will verify it. I have not had a fit since I commenced taking your treatment, and I remain well and a picture of health.

"I would write you more particulars, dear Doctor, but I know your time is valuable.   Yours, gratefully

"Miss A. KELDERHOUSE."

The People's Guide.

" ELBA, Genesee Co., Feb. 27.

"Prof. R. L. HAMILTON—*Dear Sir :* I feel that it is due to you,
as well as to all persons afflicted with disease, that I express my gratitude to you for the great benefit which I have received from the use
of your medicines. For some fifteen or twenty years my liver was in
a very bad state, and my whole system was generally debilitated. I
had been troubled with dizziness of the head so badly that at times it
was difficult for me to stand upright, and I had a blindness periodi-
cally, with a continual headache. My feet and hands were cold and
lifeless, and for about a year I had been greatly afflicted with inflam-
matory rheumatism. When I commenced taking your remedies I
could not close my hands nor raise them to my head. While in this
condition I saw your advertisement in a newspaper, giving the symptoms of a deranged liver. I had most all of those symptoms. I was,
therefore, induced to write to you, and state my case. I did so, and
received your reply. I was sensible of the fact that unless I had
help soon, there would be none in my case. In view of this, and by
the advice of a friend, I ordered a package of your medicines, and
took them as you directed. In two days I was very much relieved,
and continued to mend. I sent you the money and received a second
package, and before I had taken all of it I felt well. In about three
weeks I had gained TWENTY POUNDS of flesh, and felt the vigor of
youth. I had not felt that before in twenty years. Physicians here
said that I never could be cured of rheumatism; but it is now four
years that I have not been troubled with it. I am now about fifty-
four years old, and am able to labor hard every day. I have reason
to thank God that I learned of you, for the cure of my case was a remarkable one. I can most cheerfully recommend you to the afflicted,
and have on several occasions done so. Many of my acquaintances
have been under your treatment, and been entirely cured by your
remedies.   Truly yours,
                                          " M. HOLLISTER."

" *Genesee County*, ss. : M. Hollister, of Elba, in said county, being sworn, says that the facts set forth in the above statement are
true.   M. HOLLISTER.

" Sworn to before me, this 27th day of February, 1867.
                          " H. STILLWELL, Justice of the Peace."

A Lady Recommends Them.

Mrs. Mary A. Copeland, of North Pitcher, Chenango county, New
York, writes :

" Your medicines have worked wonders in my case. Since using
them my general health has been good, and I am able to work quite
hard. I have faith in your remedies, and can, with pleasure, recommend them to all who are suffering from the want of proper medical
treatment."

Important Case of Epileptic Fits.

Read the following evidence of what my treatment has done in a case of this disease, hitherto considered incurable:

"BUCKHART, Ill.

"Dr. HAMILTON: My wife was afflicted with fits for ten years, attended with great spinal and nervous debility. She doctored with several physicians, but all to no purpose. I read one of your circulars, and was so impressed with your new and simple theory of disease that I determined to try your remedies. As you know, we sent for your remedies, which, with the help of God, have completely and permanently cured her. She has not had a fit since, her back is strong, and her nervous vitality and strength have returned. As every attack she had was severer than the one previous, it is reasonable to suppose she could not have lived long but for the timely interference of your wonderful skill. To God be the praise! for so speedily and miraculously have your remedies worked that I can but recognize you as an instrument of Divine power in rescuing my dear companion from a terrible death. Words can but inadequately express my gratitude and joy. I wish you to publish this, and spread it far and near. I deem it my solemn duty to all afflicted with this awful malady to do all in my power to make known to them the true physician; and if any doubt the authenticity of this, let them write to me; I will satisfy them that it is all true. May God's blessing attend you in your efforts for humanity's good!

"JOHN S. SHARP."

You Have Been the Means of Saving my Life.

"WESTFIELD, N. Y.

"Dr. HAMILTON—*Dear Sir:* I have used nearly all the medicine you sent me, and herewith I inclose the money for another package. I think you will find few cases more obstinate than mine was. My bowels and back were weak and in a bad state, and many of my weak points seemed to be there. I had a very severe time with my head. I was so nervous and seemingly deranged at times that I got little or no rest for several weeks. I am much better now, and I feel almost free from disease. I think one more package of your remedies will complete the cure. But you will hear from me again, for you have been the means, under the blessing of Providence, of saving my life. My faith is fully established, and I think I understand your theory, and believe you are able to cope with any disease to which the human system is heir or liable. I had tried every other means and every other physician that I had faith in, and when all had failed to benefit me, the Lord, by some special means, directed me to you, and from the first I had faith to believe that you could cure me. In fact, I have not for many years felt so well and free from disease as I now do.

"Truly, your life-long friend,

"SIMEON McCORD."

Rheumatism—An Awful Case!!

William H. Nellis, Oleopolis, Venango County, Penn., writes:

"I return my sincere thanks for having permanently cured me of rheumatism, after having suffered severely for about seven years. When I had doctored with other doctors, and tried all the patent medicines that I could get, with no avail, and was so bad that I could not get out of my house, and part of the time not able to get out of my bed, as I was affected in nearly every joint, I thought I would try you as a last resort. To my great joy, in less than three weeks I was able to go out and jump with the most active man in the place. In one month I was perfectly cured, and had gained seventeen pounds, and I never had better health in my life."

How Grateful the Restored.

"FRENCHTOWN, Hunterdon Co., N. J."

"Dear Sir: The medicines I received from you I have taken as directed, and I cannot express my gratitude for the great benefit derived from their use. My disease is entirely, and, I believe, permanently removed. I deem it providential that I was directed to you after all other means had failed. Depend upon it, I shall do all in my power to direct poor diseased mortals to the source of relief, which, from experience, I know to be a true one. I thank you, my dear doctor, for your faithful attention, and you shall always have my best wishes for your success in relieving the suffering of your fellow-creatures. Most respectfully,
"Mrs. CHARLES BURKIT."

Rheumatism Cured.

Mr. Charles Sherman, of Rutland, Tioga County, Pa., writes:

"My rheumatism, I think, is cured. Your medicine cured my wife of Catarrh, and also helped her other complaints."

A Good Word from Maine.

Mr. S. S. Woodman, of Cornville, Somerville County, Me., writes:

"I was, one year ago, one of your patients, and took your most valuable medicines. Before I applied to you I had taken so much 'doctor stuff' that I feared no kind would do me good. The severe pains I used to have in my back and left shoulder are entirely gone. My naturally weak and feeble constitution has been built up, and (if I may be allowed to use the expression) I am an entirely new man. All this has been brought about by your truly effectual remedies. They have done for me more than I could have expected."

The Medicine was Good.

A. J. Noble, Esq., Iowa City, Iowa, writes:

"*Dear Doctor:* The medicines sent were duly received, and had the desired effect in restoring my health, with much satisfaction to myself and friends. My reason for not writing you sooner was, because I was waiting to see the result, if it would be lasting, and I am happy to inform you that I continue to feel myself a sound, hearty man, thanks to your great skill and success. I have some of the medicines still left. They are so very powerful that a little goes a long ways. I feel strong and cheerful now, eat hearty and sleep sound. I will send all the afflicted to you that I can."

Another Raised Almost from the Dead.

"Dr. HAMILTON: My husband at first thought the medicine was too powerful, but he reduced the dose and continued to take it, and it helped him wonderfully, and he has continued all the time to gain in flesh and strength. He says he has not felt so well for fifteen years. He is very hearty, and his food sets well, and he can labor with ease. We feel that your remedies have saved him from the grave; his friends and neighbors look upon him as one raised almost from the grave. The family physician had given him up to die. There are very many in our community that have great confidence in your skill, on account of your curing Mr. Park, when it seemed his case was so hopeless. May you long live to bless suffering humanity.

"Very respectfully,

"JERUSHA W. PARK.

"PITCHER, N. Y."

Entirely Restored.

"Dr. HAMILTON: Thinking you would like to hear from me, I write to let you know how my health is. My health steadily improved until I was quite well, thanks to your most excellent treatment. The disease is entirely removed, and I can never thank you as I ought for all that you have done for me. I can freely recommend you to all whom I may meet. May your life be spared long to do good, and may the blessing of God ever rest upon you, is the wish of   Yours, respectfully,

"ANNIE M. GIBSON HARGRAVES.

"TOWNSEND CENTER, Mass."

A Hopeless Case Restored.

"CHATTANOOGA, Tenn.

"Dr. HAMILTON: Kind and honored friend, this being my birth-day, which makes me fifty-three years old, I will give you the result of your treatment in my case about thirteen months ago. I was so weak—and my mind was as weak as my body—I was hardly able to write at all. I was scarcely able to get around; I felt that if you could not cure me, there was no help for me, as I had tried so many medicines, all to no effect. Sleep had almost left me; I did not draw a breath without pain. To sum it up in a few words, my case was a hopeless one, as I thought; but, thanks to your skill, I now enjoy life again. I eat hearty, I rest well at night, and continue well. If I should ever have sickness again, you shall hear from me. And now, may the blessings of our Heavenly Father ever attend you through life, and spare you to a good old age, to administer to the wants of suffering humanity, is the prayer of your friend ever,
.   "CYNTHIA L. HAIR.'

Epileptic Fits Cured.

"DALEVILLE, Lauderdale Co., Miss.

"Dr. R. L. HAMILTON—*Dear Sir:* I am happy to inform you that your medicine was received and used as directed, in the case of my son, who was afflicted with Epileptic Fits. Twelve months ago, after trying other doctors, I was induced to write to you, and received your answer and medicine; the result was a happy one. Thank God, he has remained well. I delayed writing, to see if it would hold out; he has not had a fit since. If any doubt this, tell them to write to me, and I will prove the fact.

"I am yours, with great respect,
"G. B. WHITE."

The Only Genuine Friend.

"Dr. HAMILTON: The only genuine friend I ever had, for such I feel you have been to me, for I was so near death's door when your remedies snatched me from the fell destroyer, as it were, and placed me on a firmer foundation than I had been for years. It seems to me you are certainly an instrument of God's mercy, placed here for the benefit of suffering mortals. And, verily, you will get your reward. Well, doctor, I have enjoyed better health this winter than I have for fifteen years, and feel that I am perfectly cured in every part. Indeed, I tell my acquaintances that what Dr. Hamilton doesn't know isn't worth knowing.   Your friend,
"Mrs. RACHEL OTT.

"HAVANA, Mason Co., Ill."

Sore Eyes Cured.

"About fifteen months ago I wrote to you concerning my little daughter, who was afflicted with Scrofulous Sore Eyes, and had been for some years, and it was thought by all who knew her that she would be blind in a short time, as my family physician said he could do nothing for her. You sent me remedies, which she took as directed; and in one week from the time she began to take them, her eyes began to improve, and by the time she had finished taking them she was perfectly well. I then thought I would wait through the warm weather of summer, and the changeable winter and spring, to see what effect it would have on her, before I wrote to you again; and I now feel it would be ungrateful if I did not tell you and the world that the cure was complete, and that hot or cold weather does not affect them. They are clear and strong. My neighbors, who at first hooted at me for sending to you, look upon it as almost a miracle, for all believed she was doomed to blindness. You have my grateful thanks and my prayers, and I would urgently recommend those suffering from scrofula, to apply to Dr. Hamilton at once.

"JOHN L. KEITH.

"FREELANDVILLE, Knox Co., Ind."

Your Remedies are Invaluable.

"Prof. R. L. HAMILTON—*My Dear Sir:* I shall ever feel thankful to God that I was, in His providence, directed to you, after all other means had failed to arrest the disease with which I had been suffering for six years; and I had despaired of ever being relieved, when I accidentally, humanly speaking (but I regard it all providential), saw your advertisement, and resolved to try you as the last resort. Truly your remedies are invaluable. The relief I realized has proved to be as permanent as it was magical. When I had taken the medicines sent but three weeks, I experienced a decided change, and I was encouraged to continue until I was able to leave my bed and resume my place in my family, in the enjoyment of good health, of which privilege and blessing I had been so many years deprived.

"Nearly two years have passed since my last communication to you, and I have experienced no relapse. I feel that justice demands that I should inform you of your success in the treatment of my case —of the magical and permanent effects of your remedies. Having great confidence in your skill, I can and ever will recommend you to the sick. For your kindness and faithful attention to me, allow me to remain Yours, most respectfully,

"Mrs. J. L. HART.

"DARLINGTON C. H., S. C."

Health Once More.

"Your medicines have cured me. I enjoy health once more, that boon I knew not for so many years. I shall ever feel grateful to you for these blessings, and take untold pleasure in recommending you to the afflicted ones of this earth. You are at liberty to publish any statement which I have heretofore made in your praise. I shall ever be yours, respectfully,

"NANCY BLAKEMORE.

"Kirk's Grove, Ala."

Thinks Well of Him—Can Bring the Dead Back.

E. E. Edgar, Marion Station, Miss., says:

"I feel well. I think I may say with safety, that you can come as near bringing the dead to life as can be—for my condition now and what it was proves this to me. I think more of you than any other man living, as a gentleman and a doctor, though I never saw you, and I write this from my heart."

The Right Spirit.

Mr. Samuel L. Furlong, of Muskegan, Mich., writes:

"I have cut out seventeen of the testimonials that were in the New York Tribune, and sent them to the persons themselves, with letters of inquiry about them, and also about you, and every one stated that they were true, and recommended your remedies very highly, also giving a history of their cases, which was, indeed very cheering to a poor man with a sick family."

Strong Talk.

"I received your medicines, and am a thousand times obliged to you, for you have entirely cured me of a disease which I almost thought incurable, and without your valuable treatment and advice I should have been a dead man. I would have written sooner, but I thought I would wait until I was sure that the disease was cured. You have my everlasting gratitude and esteem, dear doctor.

"Very respectfully,
"SAMUEL NESBIT.

"Waverly, Mo."

"Needs no More Medicine."

Mrs. Harriet Greenup, Smithland, Ky., says:

"I thank you kindly for the interest manifested for my recovery. I am well, and need no more medicine. If ever I should need treatment again, I will apply to you.

"Your price for treatment was so very reasonable that I can safely recommend you to both rich and poor. I will only say, as is your due, that my strength is vastly improved—my side and shoulders are well —my heart beats regularly. Many thanks to you, by the blessing of Heaven, for the cure."

A Sound Man Again.

A. F. Books, Newport, Pa., writes me to the point, thus:

"I suppose you think I ought to have taken more medicine, but the fact is, it is not necessary, as I am a sound man again. Your remedies have indeed wrought wonders in my case. Disease had to give way to your POWERFUL, YET MILD, remedies. I enjoy life once more—in fact, I am a new man. My liver and heart disease was of five years' standing, and your remedies have driven them from my system. I had been under treatment of different physicians for five long years, without deriving any benefit, until a kind Providence directed me to you. Thanking you for your kind attention and many advices, I remain yours, with a grateful heart.

"P. S.—Send me some of your pamphlets for distribution to the sick, that they may know where to apply for health like mine."

Gloom and Melancholy all Dispelled.

"NORTHFIELD, Iowa.

"Dr. HAMILTON—*My Dear Friend and Benefactor* (for such I must term you): Justice impels me to express my gratitude. It has been some time since I finished my medicine, and I have had ample time to pass from under its influence, and am most happy to say that I am sensible of a most pleasing effect. I feel very much built up generally, and the gloom and melancholy are all dispelled. Your medicines have improved me wonderfully—in fact, I can say I am reconstructed generally, both in my mental faculties and physical capacities. It is needless for me to state how well you have sustained your veracity. A most remarkable effect has been produced on my eyesight. I could not read a half hour without the letters running together and my eyes smarting; now I can read as long as I please and experience none of these unpleasant effects. I shall remember with pleasure the name of Dr. R. L. Hamilton.

"Respectfully and gratefully yours,
"JOHN McMULLEN."

Lung Trouble.

Mrs. Benjamin J. Keith, Holmes' Hole, Mass., writes:

"I feel as if I ought to write you how much good your medicines have done me. I feel a different person from what I did a year ago. I have had no return of the difficulty in my lungs or back, nor in fact any of the ill feelings I had before taking your medicine. My food never distresses me now. I thank you for your faithful attention in the past, and shall always recommend you to the afflicted; and that God may ever bless you, is my prayer."

"I am a Well Man Again."

"Prof. R. L. HAMILTON—*Dear Sir:* Duty as well as gratitude impels me to add my testimony to your superior skill in managing complicated chronic diseases. For twenty months I don't know that I had one hour free from pain. Chronic rheumatism, liver complaint, right lung affected, bowels entirely dormant—in a word, I was sinking perceptibly each day, and had made my calculations from the past that I could not live more than one month longer. In this condition, my family urged me to try you. I had no faith. I had tried many remedies and found no relief. Why try longer? They urged, and I wrote to you. Your answer was, 'I CAN CURE YOU.' It seemed to me an idle tale. The medicines *came* to hand, and I commenced taking them on the 13th August. I was one net-work of pain from head to foot. It seemed to me that my old body was going to fall to pieces. This lasted but a few hours, and then began to subside. In about forty-eight hours my pains left me, the stiffness of my joints left, and, in a few words, HEALTH came back, and, the best of all, it REMAINS with me. Thank God, through His blessings on your skill and efforts, I AM A WELL MAN AGAIN. May Heaven's choicest blessing rest upon you, my dear doctor; may you long live to bless your race.

"Should any sufferer doubt this testimony, let him write to me, or to my friends that have known me in my afflictions and since my recovery. I would refer them to

Hon. N. J. Wallace, Recorder U. S. Land Office, Dakotah Territory.
Hon. A. Carpenter, Vermilion, Clay County, " "
Peter Jourdan, Esq., " " " " "
James Curtis, Esq., Postmaster Liberty " "
E. M. Northrop, " Elk Point, Union Co., " "
E. Morris, Recorder, " " " " " "
and let them write to me for proofs.

"Yours truly, my dear doctor,

"JAMES C. DAMON.

"ELK POINT, Union Co., Dakotah Territory."

A Little Boy's Life Saved.

"CLARKSVILLE, Arkansas.

"Dr. R. L. HAMILTON—*Most Worthy Sir :* I am happy to inform you that my little boy, that you treated, is now healthy and fleshy, is running every where lively and playful. My wife joins me in the most sincere gratitude, for saving the life of our dear boy—for your medicine has, by Divine Providence, saved him.

"Ever and truly yours,

"J. J. ADAMS."

"I should be very much pleased to receive your steel-plate likeness, as I recollect with emotions of gratitude the time I solicited the attention and treatment of Doctor Hamilton, in my case. It was a success, for all of which I retain a grateful sense.

"CAROLINE MATISON.

"BARRE CENTER, Orleans Co., N. Y."

Dreadful Catarrh Cured.

"I shall forever feel grateful for the cure you have made in my case—the cure of that dreadful catarrh.

"Yours, truly,

"ELLA M. RACKLIFF.

"SAINT MARY'S, Ga."

"MEAFORD P. O., Ontario, Canada.

"Prof. HAMILTON—*Dear Sir :* I should have answered your letter long ere this, but I am feeling so well I thought it was not necessary to send for more medicine. I thought I would delay writing to you to see if my health continued good, and I am happy to tell you that I have not felt better for five or six years back ; and, sir, accept my sincere thanks. I feel very grateful to you, and hope you may long live to help the afflicted. I know that if I had not seen your advertisement, I should not be living to-day. I had been afflicted for a very long time, but now, by the blessing of God and your aid, I hope to push along well.

"You may depend upon it, if any thing goes wrong with me or mine, you will hear from me again. I do all I can for you with the sick and afflicted around here, and, in conclusion, I would ask you to accept the gratitude of your obedient servant,

"I. P. ANDERSON."

Willis Clark, West Nassau, N. Y., says:

"There can be no doubts about your skill; for it shows for itself."

Joseph H. Kirby, Berwick, Warren Co., Ill., says:

" My own health continues most excellent, and so does my family's, thank God. I still feel grateful to you for the great benefit you have done me."

A. D. Kendall, Esq., Cistern, Fayette Co., Texas, says:

"I address you as a friend, because you have proved yourself so to me."

Asbury Easter, High Hill, Montgomery Co., Mo., says:

"It is now many months since I quit taking your medicine, and am still feeling perfectly well—a thousand thanks to you."

Cures are Permanent—Read this from an Old Patient.

"I feel that it will not be out of place for me to report myself, at least once a year. I am so well, and feel that, under God, I owe so much to you, that I am impelled to continually acknowledge the same.

"CORNELIA A. VAN VLIET.

" JERICHO, Vermont."

Doubts Removed.

James Merrison, London City, Fayette Co., Ill., says:

"All doubt of you, as a successful doctor, with me, disappeared with the pain in my head and breast. These are simple facts."

Suffering Reader.

If you are afflicted with any chronic disease, throw aside, for once, any preconceived, erroneous notions in regard to an advertising physician, who gives ample evidence of his skill and integrity.

A Few Words to Our Patrons.

OUR TERMS.—Sometimes people say, "Why do you have pay in advance? Why not cure us, and then we will pay you?" A large proportion of our patients live hundreds of miles from us, and are entire strangers; and our only protection is to receive the pay before we send the medicine. No mercantile house in New York would esteem it a safe business to send goods on credit to strangers, and we must make our business safe. Our expenses are immense; our medicines are procured without reference to cost; we only use the best, let the cost be what it may. We invest in our business a large fortune every year. Our responsibility has now been tested for twenty-five years. Is it unreasonable to invest a few dollars in an enterprise which interests your health, and perhaps your life? In this way we treat all alike, impartially; we devote all our energies and study to do them the utmost good; and we depend for our patronage upon our success in curing the sick, fully realizing that we confer a blessing untold upon those we cure, and that such cures increase our business and our permanent success. Humanity prompts us to do the very best that is possible, and every testimonial we ever published is strictly reliable, as any one may ascertain by writing to the parties who have given them.

PRICES.—Our prices are not high for the services we render and the medicines supplied; and it is entirely inconsistent to always charge the same price for a supply of medicines. Of course, some cases require a greater quantity of medicine, or more expensive medicines, than others; and even when the medicines are precisely the same, the time required to make up an opinion, from the letter sent us, may be twice as great in one case as in another. We must consider each case long enough to form an accurate and reliable opinion of its nature, and also of the best medicines for that case.

WHY DO YOU ADVERTISE?—Some physicians profess to believe that it is not professional to advertise, and the above question is sometimes asked us. We advertise:

1st. Because it makes our enterprise known, and thousands who have been cured by our medicines have thus first learned of us. Advertising multiplies our opportunities to cure the afflicted a hundredfold. This reason is all-sufficient to any person who has a spark of humanity.

2d. Because it is honorable. Some maintain that it is not honorable to advertise, because "quacks advertise." Villains intrude into every kind of society, but that is no reason why we should not belong to any organization which we deem to be useful, honorable, and humane. The more useful and honorable the enterprise, the more ought it to be made known to mankind.

8d. Because it pays us, and we pay for it, and have a mind to advertise. We choose to put our enterprise on record before the people, and we approve of encouraging every man to act independently, provided only that he does what he thinks is right. Any "code of ethics" among half-educated and wholly selfish medical men, which would forbid this, is contrary to humanity, fifty years behind the times, and utterly unworthy of an educated, independent, and conscientious man. According to any such "code," any man who can cure cancer, consumption, or malignant diphtheria, should never make it known beyond his own circle of friends! We should consider such a course as little better than manslaughter; it would be to let people die because a selfish organization commands us "not to advertise " a skill which we know ourselves to possess.

PREPARATORY TREATMENT.—To some patients, we send a small package of a suitable medicine, as a preparatory treatment. This treatment is entirely preparatory, and patients should not wait to see that it benefits them before sending for other medicine. It only prepares the way for other treatment, and thus makes the other treatment act better and quicker. As soon as you commence taking the Preparatory Treatment, send at once for other medicines, so that you will receive the medicines as soon as you have taken the first; no time will be lost, and your system will be in a right state to be most benefited, and be surer of entire relief.

Another Appeal to the Incredulous.

So well knowing the general custom of the American people to denounce all advertising Physicians as "humbugs," without knowing anything at all in regard to their merits, that in addition to the numerous and wonderful testimonials from some of the thousands who have been cured by me, I publish below the names and addresses of a few reliable persons who know me well as a man of reliability and integrity:

John Proper, Waterford, N. Y.; Timothy Cronin, Attorney-at-law, No. 161 Broadway, New York city; J. M. Emerson, No. 83 Nassau

street, New York city; Norval M. White, Clerk
Post-office; Dr. Palmer, No. 78 Fourth avenue, Ne
ward Burlingame, Troy, N. Y.; Harvey Wilcox, F
G. W. Lord, Attorney-at-law, No. 55 Liberty stree
Charles Van Benthuysen & Sons, State Printers, /
seph Anderson, No. 81 Adams street, Brooklyn, N.
Sandford, N. Y.; Daniel Edwards, Otego, N. Y.; M
bury, N. Y.; Thomas Colby, Moresville, N. Y.; The
ville, N. Y.; A. B. Sands & Co., Druggists, No. 141 W
York city; Wm. Youngblood, No. 83 Nassau stree
John E. Van Etten, Attorney-at-law, Kingston, N.
ton, Stamford, N. Y.; Henry Biers, Chicago, Ill.; (
Druggists, No. 108 John street, N. Y.

It must be remembered that the above are all g(
ness men, to whom any one may refer by letter or of
reliability and honesty of myself as a man of bu

Further Evidence.

Below I give a list of responsible persons who hav
treated by me with great success, any one of whom
questions by letter or in person, in regard to my tr
cases. Had I the space, and were it possible, I woul
tory and character of each case in full. Some of
wonderful cures. But for want of space I can onl;
a general way. I do this to give the skeptical all tl
power of my reliability and remarkable skill. I fu
tinctly understood that I DO NOT CLAIM TO CURE ALL (
sonable people must realize that there is a *point* in
tions which no *human aid* can reach, however wel
may be directed. In many instances of these grav
physician can do *much* to soothe the pathway to the
correspondingly elevate the undeveloped spirit, and
pare it for a higher existence.

Tuthill Carter, Esq., Atlanticville, N. Y.; Mrs.
York Mills, N. Y.; W. C. Porter. Millwood, Mo.; Sa1
Esq., Dillsbury, Penn.; Ann C. Bradford, Potter, :
Whipple. Cambridge, Vt.; Mrs. Sue J. F. Barnett, P;
Emily W. Reid, Ellicottville, N. Y.; L. E. Fish, Esq.
Ella M. Rackliff, St. Mary's, Ga.; Sabina E. Olds, W(
A. Pickett, Esq., Jacksonville, Fla.; Louisa O. Cobb
Adam Grubb, Louisville, Ala.; J. L. Higbee, Esq., C;
Francis E. Wood, Esq., New Road, N. Y.; Alice Emo1

N. Y.; Mrs. H. A. Taylor, East Troy, Wis.; Mrs. Mary E. Mitchell, Jersey Shore, Penn.; Mrs. Abirah Dedrich, Sterlingville, Penn.; J. H. Spencer, Sugar Grove, Ky.; Wm. Freeburn, Latrobe, Neb.; Herman Hearlein, Esq., Atlanta, Ga.; J. M. Vansyckle, Esq., Wallula, Washington Territory; Wm. Walker, Esq., Wellington, Iowa; Edward Hutchinson, Esq., Chatsworth, Ill.; P. Schermerhorn, Bloomville, N. Y.; Mrs.J. Laidlow, box No. 703, Fort Wayne, Ind.; Marion A.Crandall, Nile, N. Y.; E. Kate Rodney, Coatesville, Penn.; Mrs. E. W. Chase, Warsaw, N. Y.; M. S. Hamilton, Pine Bluff, Ark.; Mrs. C. M. Welsh, Farmer City, Ill; Miss Mattie Lawrence, North Leominster, Mass.; Wm. Smith, Esq., P. O. box No. 53, Portland, Me.; N. E. Hicks, Wetumka, Ala.; J. J. Bisel, Lock Haven, Penn.; Mrs. Samuel Sawyer, Grout's Corners, Mass.; Lizzie B. Harris, Winchester, Mass.; Rev. Washington Medaris, Sidney, Ohio; Mrs. H. Garrett, Kansas City, Mo.; Benjamin Berry, Esq., Matteawan, N. Y.; Alexander Hughes, Esq., Poughkeepsie, N. Y. ; Wm. B. Betts, Esq., Norwich, Conn. ; S. S. Parker, Esq., Alabama, N.Y.; Luke Newell, Mason, N. H.; Mollie A. Brooks, West Point, Ga.; Mrs. S. E. Blackwell, Cokesbury, S. C.; Mrs. A. S. Childs, Richmond, Mo.; H. Houghton, LaGrange, Wis.; Mrs. D. Eggleston, Locust Hill, Mo.; Mr. E. J. Ireland, Shattuckville, Mass; Mr. W. W. Pence, Indian Creek, W. Va.; Sarah Walker, Forest City, Mo.; Mr. Moses Tewell, Elbensville, Pa.; Mrs. D. M. Harber, Mackville, Ky.; Cordelia A. Valleau, Portland, Wis.; Emeline E. Miner, Taylor, N. Y.; Mary E. Lecktness, Ainsworth, Iowa; Herman Galner, Farmers' Fork, W. Va.; Mrs. Lou. M. Richardson, Cleburne, Texas; G. Fairchild, Okoboji, Iowa; Mr. Walter Cline, Pitcher, N. Y.; Betsey Richman, Manlius Center, N. Y.; Peleg S. Curtiss, Deer Isle, Me.; A. H. Thumbo, Lynchburg, Ohio; W. G. Fowler, Wilmington, N. C ; Mrs. L. R. Dyer, Grant, N. Y.; Mr. Irwin Seward, New Providence, Iowa; Hannah M. Coffee, Rural, Ill.; M. V. Babcock, Auburn, N. Y.; Miss Mary W. Perry, Sandersville, Ga.; Mrs. F. Ballaine, Peverly, Mo.; L. D. Colbert, Esq., Washington, Ind.; Mr. J. N. Barnett, Shabonier, Ill.; Mrs. Phebe L. Vance, Sun Prairie, Wis.; Rev. W. R. Black, Fredonia, Kansas; Rev. A. C. Shepherdson, Three Rivers, Mich.; Mrs. Joseph Vallett, Batavia, N. Y.; Mr. O. E. Russel, Middleport, Ohio; Mr. A. Searles, Jr., Schaghticoke, N. Y.; M. M. Clark, West Farmington, O.; S. H. Burch, Hiawasse, Ga.; Mr. David Holman, Stockton, Pa.; Miss Louisa J. Russel, Bonus, Ill.; Mr. W. H. Cambridge, Pebble Creek, Neb.; Mary Ann Lawrence, St. Johnsbury, Vt.; Harriet Briggs, Brush's Mills, N. Y.; Mr. J. C. Prentiss, Ravenna, O.; S. D. Lounsbury, Rensselaerville, N. Y.; Indiana Neville, Batavia, Iowa; A. A. Slater, Essex, Vt.; Mary Green, North Brookfield, Mass.; Angeline Phelps, Pine Valley, Pa.; Rev. Thomas Sugg, Waco, Ala.; Nelus P. Nelson, Bedford, Iowa; James S. McCall, Society Hill, S. C.; Mrs. Marcus F. Spaulding, Newark Valley, N. Y.; Mrs. Rachel Ott, Havana, Ill.; A. H. Duncan, Sparta, Tenn.; John W. Keeler, Oakland City, Ind.; Mattie I. Thomas, Pottersville, N. J.; Rachel McElroy, Millwood, Ohio; Edward G. Miner, Great Barrington, Mass., Albert G. Fay, Geneseo, Ill.; B. F. Ward, Indian Springs, Ga.; Rev. J. H. Fesperman, Salisbury, N. C. ; N. J. Ackerman, Orwell,

N. C.; Mrs. T. F. Rantz, Quasqueton, Buchanan Co., Iowa; Samuel Russell, West Union, W. Va.; C. S. Markwood, Esq., Lancaster, Ohio; Miss L. E. Fanshawe, Darien Depot, Conn.; I. D. W. Bowman, Esq., Havana, Ill.; Jas. D. Pease, Esq., Trumansburg, N. Y.; Mrs. Daniel Berry, Greenland, N. H.; Wm. Humes, New Castle, Pa.; Miss M. Atchison, Mendon, Mich.; George Shaw, Port Severn P. O., Ontario, Canada; Mrs. Jesse Walker, Mattole, Humboldt Co., Cal.; Miss Kezia Rosenberry, Upper Strasbourg, Pa.; Sidney A. A. Clark, Harrison, Tenn.; Lizzie J. Graham, Cumberland Mills, Portland, Me.; Mrs. A. J. Horton, Eddyville, Iowa; Mrs. Geo. H. Trowbridge, Litchfield, Conn.; John C. Calhoun, Greenwich, Washington Co., N. Y.; C. Fairchild, Esq., Editor "*Ovid Bee*," Ovid, N. Y.; Samuel Messick, Esq., Seaford, Del.; Henry Doyle, Scranton, Pa.; J. P. Cole, Weston, Lewis Co., W. Va.; A. B. Day, Galva, Ill.; H. A. McDonald, Bremond, Texas; E. Olmstead, North Wilton, Conn.

How to Send Money.

In remitting by *draft or check*, you have to pay the premium, or I have to pay the expense of collection, which *I will not do.*

In remitting by *money order*, it is true that if the money order is lost, a duplicate can be procured; but this method involves so much DELAY that it generally takes from two to five weeks, according to distance, and all this time you are waiting for your medicine. The reason for this is, because after you notify your Postmaster that the order is lost, he has to write to the New York Postmaster certifying to the fact; then the latter afterwards writes to the Post-Office Department at Washington, and after all this the Department at Washington sends me a duplicate, and then I get the money. This, you see, takes a long time, even if attended to at once and no more mistakes happen to be made. I know of cases where it has taken as long as six months in getting this very plain business through, just owing to a simple mistake.

In sending by *express*, you have to pay largely for express charges (which in every instance must be prepaid, as I will not pay the charges on money sent to me), and, although good as regards security, is more expensive than by *registered letter*, which only costs fifteen cents from any Post-Office in the country.

Registered Letters.

The reasons why I advise the sending of your money to me in a registered letter are as follows:

1st. Its CHEAPNESS—only fifteen cents.

2d. Its SECURITY. When a registered letter is delivered to me, I have to sign a receipt for it, which is sent back to your Postmaster, whose duty by law is to give this receipt to you upon its arrival in his office; and thus you can know with certainty if I have received the money, and not until then am I responsible for it.

3d. Its RAPIDITY. Meeting with no express agents' delays, no banker's inspection, it does not have to be negotiated or collected: IT IS the money.

In conclusion, I would say: Put your money carefully in the letter; put fifteen cents in postage stamps on it, besides the postage; take it to the Postmaster, and obtain from him (as the law requires), a "registered letter receipt." When the letter containing the money is given to me, I sign a receipt for it or I cannot get it, which latter receipt is forwarded to you, as before stated, and is your property, and if your Postmaster does not give it to you, it is presumptive evidence that the money has been stolen. You thus obtain two receipts, one from the Postmaster that he will send it, and one from me afterward (through him), that I have received it. NEVER send money in a letter without registering it, and ALWAYS procure BOTH of the receipts mentioned. If you do this strictly, there will be no trouble, vexation, or delay.

The postmaster is under the obligations of his oath of office, to register your letter when you ask him. He can be reported to the Postmaster General at Washington if he refuses, and removed from his office.

☞ *All Letters for Prof. Hamilton should be addressed thus:*

R. L. HAMILTON, M.D.,
Box No. 4952,
NEW YORK CITY.

Reader:

One moment, if you please, and we have done! You, who are now languishing upon beds of sickness and suffering, give ear to common sense for one brief moment, and let us reason together for your own welfare and happiness.

First: Have you carefully read the theory put forward in the first of this article? Does it stand the test of your own reason? Do any of the symptoms apply to your own case; and if not, wherein do they fail? Does Dr. HAMILTON not give ample evidence of his skill to those who are afflicted with chronic disease, as treated by him with such unparalleled success for over a quarter of a century? What, in all reason and justice, can you require MORE to convince you of his superior skill as a physician, and of his integrity and honor as a man? It is certainly foolish and out of place to cry humbug in this matter. Can you, for one moment, believe that ALL of the good, honorable, respectable and well-known business men whose names are given above as references, are imaginary men? or that their names have been published by Dr. HAMILTON to advance his own interests, as an impostor, to gull the people? Do you dare to cry "Quack" and "Humbug," after reading the strong testimonials which are published in this article, from reliable persons, who have themselves been saved from suffering and death by Dr. HAMILTON's remarkable skill.

Is it not wisdom and justice to consider all men honorable till they have been proved otherwise? Is it good reason to turn a deaf ear to all appeals of eminent physicians who give undisputable evidence of their skill and integrity, although you may have never before heard of them?

It must be understood that all who have sent to Dr. H. their testimonials for publication as above, are good, honest, reliable, and substantial people, who can at any and all times be seen or written to in regard to the truth or falsity of the testimonials. Hundreds of others could be published had we the space, all of which are real, genuine, truthful evidences of what Dr. H. has done, and is still doing daily. Again we will say, that in no instance has Dr. H. asked or solicited testimonials from his patients; all that are published are gratuitous contributions, sent with a request that *they may be published for the benefit of the sick and suffering*, and for no other purpose.

Remember One Thing ! ! !

Reader, do you think that you cannot be cured because you have tried other remedies and they have failed. It will be understood from my remarks, in various places in the foregoing pages, that many of my remedies are known only to myself, for many of them are discoveries of my own, and are compounded according to my own reasoning and extensive experience with the sick.

All sick persons will observe that if they wish to be put upon a course of treatment which will cure them, they can write me their present symptoms, plainly; or patients can mark the symptoms they have, as published on page 27 of this pamphlet. I can, in every instance, prescribe for them just as well as though I saw them, for I have, constantly, thousands under my treatment, in various parts of the world, whom I never see, all of whom I cure as speedily and safely as those I see in person—in fact, some of the best cures I ever made I perfected in cases I never saw.

All I wish to know, in any case, is the most prominent symptoms; and they can just as well be written as told to a physician, and I can treat the case as easily as though the patient were present.

All invalids afflicted with the diseases referred to, or with any form of chronic disease, can write me at once, and I will answer you promptly and to the point, and state fully the facts as they appear, and whether you can or cannot be saved. Do not give up, even though your family physician has done you no good ; for I have saved thousands after all hope had fled and the grave was near. The wisdom and goodness of a just Providence will not withhold the noble means for the restoration and cure of his suffering and erring children.

Also, if you expect a full and specific reply to your letter, always inclose ten cents. Postage must be paid in advance, and all persons under treatment who write us for advice, or any other purpose, must inclose with each letter ten cents, to pay for postage and time ; for it must be borne in mind that " time is money," and having so many letters of the kind every day, it consumes one-half of our time.

R. Leonidas Hamilton, M.D.,

is a thoroughly educated physician, a regular graduate of our best medical schools, a man of over twenty-five years' experience in all chronic diseases to which the people of this or any country are subject, who has at this moment patients under treatment in every State and Territory of the American Union, in the British Provinces, South and Central America, Mexico, West Indies, and Sandwich Islands, Europe, China, and the East. This will doubtless sound chimerical to many, but the evidence can be produced at Dr. II.'s office to prove every word true. It is also asserted, on the most reliable authority, that no one physician in this or any other country on the globe, of whatever age or position, has ever seen, examined, and prescribed for, one-half the number of patients that Dr. HAMILTON has. Again, it must not be supposed that Dr. HAMILTON's treatment consists in *Patent Medicines* or a *few pet compounds*, recommended to cure all the ills that flesh is subject to. On the contrary, Dr. II.'s prescriptions and specific compounds are always made up, chemically and specifically, for each individual case, as they are presented to him, either in person or by letter—either of which is sufficient, if the combination of symptoms are properly presented, according to the directions given below or elsewhere in this article.

Again : No MINERAL remedies are used in any case by Dr. HAMILTON ; consequently patients are safe from those horrible mineral poisons so much used by some physicians.

Conclusion.

It would seem to us that, after carefully looking over the evidence given in these pages, all reasonable persons must be led to the conclusion that there can be no good reason for doubting the fact that Dr. HAMILTON is just what he is represented to be—a very successful physician in the treatment of Chronic Diseases. It is useless to cry "Humbug!" for the patients who have been cured, and whose testimonials are here presented, have *volunteered* to give their evidence for the benefit of the suffering, and for no other purpose. All these testimonials are genuine—are guaranteed to be so, in fact; and it is easy to write to them, and get from their own pen the FACTS. Any of them will answer all inquiries of this character.

Have no hesitation in writing to me, and state to me your case in full, and I will deal honestly and promptly with you.

All letters to me must be addressed thus:

R. L. HAMILTON, M.D.,

Box No. 4952,

NEW YORK CITY.

The number of the Post-office Box must be put on each letter, to secure safety.

--- ◄◆► ---

DR. HAMILTON'S OFFICE

IS AT

546 BROADWAY.

PART SECOND.

FACTS FOR THE PEOPLE !

Food that Makes Brains.

It may be asked if the characteristics of branial food do not vary so much as to preclude the formation of any reliable judgment in the selection of our diet. By no means, for, though our data is not so complete as is desirable, theory and practice have established much that is most profoundly valuable and altogether worthy of reliance. It is, indeed, of no small importance to establish that some kinds of food, even if we do not know them, must be more valuable than others for nourishing the brain—for, the general principle being acknowledged, the minds of thinking men will not rest till it has been made applicable.

The next step is, however, to notice the undeniable and easily substantiated fact, that with each mental action, either sensation, emotion, intellection, or volition, there is associated, either as cause or effect, or as concomitant, a decomposition of a corresponding portion of the brain. Whenever there is a great mental activity, the earthly matter removed by the kidneys will be invariably greatly increased, which fact is noticeable by any one, however he may account for it. These phosphates do arise from the brain, where they are taken into the blood, from which they are eliminated by the kidneys. The substance of the brain thus removed must be replaced; hence, a suggestion of hunger will be caused. It is, however, a different sensation from that usually so called. This arises from a necessity to provide against the effects of cold and of muscular exercise, and is experienced from the earliest periods of life. The sensation caused by the demands of the brain partakes more of the feeling of exhaustion that some readily, and others never, learn to recognize as hunger. It is easily and only satisfied by eating the right kinds of food, that seem at once to "go directly to the spot." Our tables are usually supplied with food that experience testifies will satisfy a caloric and muscular appetite, and science justifies the arrangement, since there is a sufficient amount of the kind that the ordinary activity of the brain requires. But when a greater activity of the brain produces a different kind of hunger, requiring a different kind of food, or a larger proportion of one class of it, the mind has had time or age to become informed in regard to the nature and structure constituted for its development, and should know how to observe and interpret the corporeal signals, and how to supply the materials for the special repairs of the body. But, alas! men have been so busy with the introspection of mental development and phenomena, by means of consciousness, that they have forgotten to trace the relations of mind to the body. Thus the mechanism becomes more and more exhausted, and they have not the ability to revivify it, from a want of the knowledge of material conditions upon which continued mental action depends.

The pith of the whole matter, then, is this: The ordinary food of our tables is composed of the elements required for producing heat, renewing muscles, supplying secretions, and maintaining the ordinary repairs of the brain. The man, however, who is exposed to extreme cold weather, finds his appetite demands large quantities of fat, or food corresponding in its powers of producing heat; so the man who is freely perspiring has often a return of thirst; and the man who vigorously exercises his muscles cannot endure without corresponding hearty food. The same idea must be and is true of the man who is exercising his brain actively for hours together; he must either eat enormously of the kinds of food that contain but little of the kind he requires, which is injudicious—or, which is more proper, he must select for his use those kinds of food in which the material best adapted for his use abounds.

What kinds are they? is the very question with which we started upon our inquiry.

We know that from the contents of an egg-shell all the parts of a chicken are constructed. The shell must, therefore, contain the elements of brain properly conditioned to be readily wrought into it. The experience of ages testifies that in cases of nervous debility, "a raw egg before breakfast" is particularly strengthening. It may be thought to be, because taken as a medicine. But, in fact, it is an easily digested branial food. Indeed, at almost any price per dozen, eggs, taken in reasonable numbers, if properly cooked, are not only the best, but the cheapest kind of meat that can be used. Eggs, however, afford a particularly good example of the different value of articles called by the same name. Those with light-colored yolks are not so rich for cake, nor so good for man, as those with deep-colored yolks. Duck eggs are particularly rich. The eggs of hens fed upon bugs, worms, grasshoppers, and upon fish, are deeper colored and richer than those of fowls fed upon corn, etc. This leads to the remark, that many a literary man has found delicious refreshment in a dish of oysters, sardines, or other fish, more particularly those that abound in phosphorescent qualities; such give great content to the stomach goaded to appetite by an exhausted brain. Now, as phosphorus has been found to abound more in the brain than in any other corporeal organ, is it not plainly shown that there is a relation between the kinds of food mentioned and the brain, and when this faithful servant asks for bread, shall we offer it a stone?

Every one who has had any thing to do with a horse, knows that he becomes a more nervously active animal if fed upon oats, than if fed upon grass or upon corn, and that "wheat will also put the life into him." Whoever, also, has had a Scotch master, scholar and companion, knows that great nervous endurance will be necessary to keep pace with the Scotch mind. Has this fact no relation to the oatmeal cakes that are a by-word for the land whence he came? All preparations of oatmeal will make Scotch metaphysics easy to take, and no other physic necessary.

Again, Graham, with his "scratch the alimentary canal" idea, brought into vogue the fashion of eating unbolted wheat, overvaluing the bran, that he thought was pregnant with virtues. Had he bolted out the bran, the bread would have been improved, since its virtues are latent in the brown part, between the bran and the white flour. The brown contains the chief part of the phosphate of the wheat, and is, for branial purposes, worth ten times as much per pound as the white flour. Indeed, the brown or middlings, or kernel, or grudgeons of the wheat, is the cheapest brain food that the market supplies. Unbolted wheat flour comes next in order, cracked wheat being in the same category. Wheat entire, boiled, or brought almost to boiling for several hours, furnishes a very delicious or wholesome food, either eaten plain, as a mush, or used as a basis for many delicious articles. The Arabs find beans an excellent food for horses, and like peas, if sufficiently cooked, so as to render them easily digested, make excellent food for the brain.

One other article may be mentioned, that it seems would so readily be recognized as adapted to branial nutrition that no mention of it would be necessary. But it is as true as strange, that nine-tenths of the American people do not make any use of the brains of animals, casting them aside as if unfit for food—which is distinctly to say they do not make full use of their own. Brains are, in fact, the most valuable per pound of any part of a creature; easily digested, they can in various ways be cooked so as to be deliciously palatable. It is certainly an *ad captandum* argument, that the brains of animals must form a useful kind of food to the man who is called upon for extraordinary branial activity. The old proverb that each part strengthens a part, would certainly apply in this case. The decisions of science and the testimony of experience agree that in this case the *ad captandum* is worthy of entire confidence. More food of this kind is believed to be thrown away in this State than would, if estimated at its real value, equal all the expenses of public education in the State.

Science, experience, and reasoning from analogy and from the nature of the case, arrive at the same conclusion in respect to the character of certain kinds of food, and the relations they sustain to the brain; and while we are thus shown what we should use for the best effect, it is highly gratifying to learn that those kinds of food that are best for the brain are also the cheapest in price, and may be prepared in several ways, so as to be most delicious to the palate.

There certainly is no need of a homily to awaken emotions of gratitude and admiration toward the Infinite Wisdom and Goodness that has thus provided food for man's good and for his enjoyment, with ease in attainment. It will also be gratifying to notice that when the cold winter is softening into the mildness of spring, and the body no longer needs the heat-producing elements that are found in oats, wheat, and other grains, the fowls bestir themselves to provide eggs for the needs of intellectual men, and immense schools of fish pour themselves along our coasts and into our rivers, inviting the net to dip them out for man's use. The wide ocean seems to be a storehouse to provide for man's intellectual development. Thus, by eggs and fish, he is in spring supplied by that which he may eat abundantly to supply all the wants of the brain, without overloading the blood with heat-producing and torpifying food. Thus it is seen that the solid framework of the earth was laid, its gigantic mountain ribs built up, its sublime ocean depths furrowed out, and even the poles turned askant, that man might feed his body with food appropriate in the various seasons for intellectual development, as well as by the grandeur and adaptation of nature directly nourish in his soul adequate notions of the Deity.

Cheap Bread.

"Bread and butter" are the only articles of food of which we never tire for a day, from early childhood to extreme old age. A pound of fine flour or Indian (corn) meal contains three times as much meat as one pound of butchers' roast beef, and if the whole product of the grain, bran and all, were made into bread, fifteen per cent. more of nutriment would be added. Unfortunately the bran, the coarsest part, is thrown away; the very part which gives soundness to the teeth, and strength to the bones, and vigor to the brain. Five hundred pounds of fine flour give to the body thirty pounds of the bony element, while the same quantity of bran gives one hundred and twenty-five pounds! This bone is "lime," the phosphate of lime, the indispensable element of health to the whole human body, from the want of the natural supply of which multitudes of persons go into a general "decline." But swallowing phosphates in the shape of powders, or in syrups, to cure these declines, has little or no virtue. The articles contained in these phosphates must pass through nature's laboratory, must be subject to her manipulations, in alembics specially prepared by Almighty power and skill, in order to impart their peculiar virtues to the human frame. In plainer phrase, the shortest, safest, and most infallible method of giving strength to the body, bone, and brain, thereby arresting disease, and building up the constitution, is to eat and digest more bread made out of the whole grain, whether of wheat, corn, rye, or oats. But we must get an appetite for eating more, and a power of digesting more. Not by the artificial and lazy method of drinking bitters and taking tonics, but by moderate, continued, and remunerative muscular exercise in the open air, every day, rain or shine. And that we may eat the more of it, the bread must be good and cheap and healthful; and that which combines these three qualities to a greater extent than any other known on the face of the globe, as far as we know, is made thus: To two quarts of corn (Indian) meal, add one pint of bread sponge; water sufficiently to wet the whole; add one-half pint of flour and a teaspoonful of salt. Let it rise; then knead well, unsparingly, for the second time. Place the dough in the oven, and let it bake an hour and a half. Keep on trying until you succeed in making a light, well-baked loaf. Our cook succeeded admirably by our directions at the very first trial. It costs just half as much as bread from the finest family flour, is lighter on the stomach, and imparts more health, vigor, and strength to the body, brain, and bone. Three pounds of such bread (at five cents a pound for the meal) afford as much nutriment as nine pounds of good roast beef (costing, at twenty-five cents, two dollars and twenty-five cents), according to standard physiological tables.

Eating Economically.

What kind of food has the most nourishment and costs the least, is a question of great practical importance. The following tables may be studied with considerable interest by every family. They will show the mode of preparation, the amount of nutriment, and the time required for the digestion of the most common articles of food placed upon our tables. A dollar's worth of meat, at twenty-five cents a pound, goes as far as fifty cents' worth of butter, at half a dollar a pound. Three pounds of flour, at eight cents a pound, are said to contain as much nutriment as nine pounds of roast beef, which, at twenty-five cents, is two dollars and a quarter; that is, twenty-five cents' worth of flour goes as far as nine times that much money spent for roast beef, as weighed at the butcher's stall. A pint of white beans, weighing one pound, and costing seven cents, contains as much nutriment as three pounds and a half of roast beef, costing eighty-seven and a half cents. Of all the articles that can be eaten, the cheapest are bread, butter, molasses, beans, and rice. A pound of corn meal

(Indian) goes as far as a pound of flour; so that, fine family flour at sixteen dollars a barrel, in New York city, in July, 1870, and corn meal at four cents, the latter is just one-half less expensive. If corn and wheat were ground, and the whole product, bran and all, were made into bread, fifteen per cent. of nutriment would be saved, with much greater healthfulness. These are standard tables:

Quantity of Food.	Mode of Preparation.	Amount of Nutriment.	Time of Digestion. M. M.
Cucumbers	Raw	2 per cent	
Turnips	Boiled	4 "	3.30
Milk	Fresh.	7 "	2.15
Cabbage	Boiled	7 "	4.30
Apples	Raw	10 "	1.50
Potatoes	Boiled	18 "	2.30
Fish	Broiled	20 "	2.00
Venison	"	22 "	1.30
Pork	Roasted	24 "	5.15
Veal	"	25 "	4.00
Beef	"	26 "	3.30
Poultry	"	27 "	2.45
Mutton	"	30 "	3.15
Bread, wheat	Baked	80 "	3.30
Bread	"	80 "	3.30
Beans	Boiled	67 "	2.30
Rice		88 "	1.00
Butter and Oils		96 "	3.30
Sugar and Syrups.		96 "	3.30

Corn Against Pork and Beef.

I believe it is not generally known that it takes about ten pounds of corn to make one pound of beef or pork. Nevertheless, it is a fact, which has been fully demonstrated by careful experiments. It is also an established fact, that one pound of corn contains more than twice as much nutritious matter as a pound of average butchers' meat. Thus butchers' meat furnishes in all only 36.6 parts in 100 of solid matter, to 63.4 of water; while corn meal contains 90 parts in 100 of solid matter, and only 10 of water.

Now, in following out and applying these facts, we arrive at conclusions that may be, to some, not a little startling. We find, for example, that the change of corn into beef and pork, especially the latter, is a most palpable violation of the laws of domestic and political economy. For if it should be taken for granted that we raise 800,000,000 bushels of corn in the United States in a year (and this is estimated to be the fact, by Mr. John Jay, of the Geographical and Statistical Society of New York), is it not safe to suppose that at least one-half of it is employed in fattening animals? And if it takes as much corn to make a pound of pork as it does to make a pound of beef, then here is a waste of 360,000,000 bushels of this valuable product: or, at fifty cents a bushel, of $180,000,000; even though we admit that a pound of beef contained as much nutritious matter as a pound of corn, which we have seen above is not true.

If it is said, as it may be, that this is a national loss rather than a loss to individuals, I should like to know how it can be made out. I see no reason why a national is not a loss to each individual making up that nation—and, in general, a loss which falls upon all about equally. If this is so, and we take our present population to be 80,000,000, here is a loss of six dollars to each individual, or thirty dollars for a family of five persons. If, however, we admit the corn to be twice as much per pound as the beef—I mean for all the purposes of human nutrition—then the loss, of course, is double that sum, or sixty dollars to a family. Are we able and willing to bear this loss? Some may say they prefer the beef and pork, because it makes them warmer than corn bread. But, if this were admitted, the difference in favor of the animal food could not be as great as ten to one. It is not to be admitted, however. Corn meal contains 77 parts in 100 of the heat-forming principle, and butchers' meat only a fraction over 14 parts in 100.

It may be said that the beef and pork taste better than the Johnnycake or the pudding. Not to the inhabitants of those countries that are sustained almost wholly on corn. Nor do they, indeed, to any one whose taste is pure and unperverted. It is a species of cannibalism in human society that makes a person relish flesh and blood, with all the filth that belongs to every part and parcel of them—some items of which it would not do, for decency's sake, to specify.

PART THIRD,

MISCELLANEOUS RECIPES.

Preserving Sinks from Foulness.

In hot weather it is almost impossible to prevent sinks becoming foul, unless some chemical preparation is used. One pound of copperas dissolved in four gallons of water, poured over the sink three or four times, will completely destroy the offensive odor. As a disinfecting agent to scatter around premises affected with any unpleasant odor, nothing is better than powdered charcoal. All sorts of glass vessels and other utensils may be effectually cured from offensive smell by rinsing them with charcoal powder, after the grosser impurities have been scoured off with sand and soap.

Chemical Action of Light.

Never shade a house. Let sunlight into every room, and let every inhabitant feel its influence. Man requires sunlight as much as plants; sunlight and fresh air are essential to health.

A Fine Cologne.

Take one quart of good alcohol, one ounce each oil lavender and oil lemon, one dram oil cinnamon, two drams extract or tincture of musk, and six drops otto of rose; mix well together. This is a fine cologne, if the ingredients are all pure and reliable.

Perfume for the Handkerchief.

Take one pint best cologne spirits, half ounce oil jessamine, one-fourth ounce oil geanium, half ounce extract of musk, or those that prefer it may add six drops of otto of rose instead; mix, and bottle tight. Very choice.

Hungarian Hair Oil.

Take four ounces each of strong alcohol and castor oil, tinct. of red sanders or alkanet half-ounce, oil bergamot, oil lavender, oil lemon, of each one dram. Mix thoroughly and bottle.

To Make Sticking Salve.

Three pounds resin, half pound of mutton tallow, half pound of beeswax, and a tablespoonful of sulphur, melted, poured into cold water, and worked and pulled an hour.

Indelible Ink for Cloth.

Take soft water two ounces, nitrate silver four drams, spirits harts-horn two drams. Mix thoroughly, then add two drams sap green, grated fine. Bottle tight, and use with a quill pen. This makes one of the most permanent and jet black indelible inks ever made. Cloth marked with this should be exposed to the strong heat of the sun half an hour, or a warm iron may be run over it.

A Receipt Worth One Thousand Dollars.

Take one pound of soda and half a pound of unslaked lime, put them in a gallon of water, and let them boil twenty minutes; let it stand till cool; then drain off, and put it in a stone jug or jar. Soak your dirty clothes over night, or until they are wet through; then wring them out and rub on plenty of soap, and in one boiler of clothes well covered with water, add one teaspoonful of the washing fluid. Boil half an hour briskly, then wash them thoroughly through one suds, and rinse well through two waters, and your clothes will look better than the old way of washing twice before boiling. This recipe is invaluable, and every poor tired woman should try it. With a patent tub to do the little rubbing, the washerwoman might take the last novel and compose herself on the lounge, and let the washing do itself.

To Prevent Hair from Falling Out.

Take one pint of cologne, two ounces tincture of bloodroot, two ounces castor oil, half an ounce tincture of Spanish fly, and half an ounce of Castile soap, grated fine. Mix thoroughly together. Apply once a day with a brush.

Remedy for Earache.

Take one teaspoonful each of the juice of grated onions and blood beet; mix and drop several drops in the ear warm; use it often. If the pain is very great, moisten wool or cotton with the same, and put it in the ear every ten minutes. Seldom fails to give instant relief.

Eye Wash for Inflammation of the Eyes.

Take half a teaspoonful of common fine salt, one-eighth teaspoonful of white vitriol, hot sage tea one teacupful, mix when cold, wet linen cloths, and apply to the eyes often. Should it smart too much at first, reduce it with rain or soft water. In all of these cases Liver Specific should be taken to cure the blood.

The Toothache.

An exchange gives the following: "My dear friend," said H., "I can cure your toothache in ten minutes." "How? how?" I inquired. "Do it in pity." "Instantly," said he. "Have you any alum?" "Yes." "Bring it, and some common salt." They were produced. My friend pulverized them, mixed them in equal quantities, then wet a small piece of cotton, causing the mixed powder to adhere, and placed it in my hollow tooth. "There," said he, "if that does not cure you I will forfeit my head. You may tell this to every one, and publish it every where. The remedy is infallible." It was as he predicted. On the introduction of the mixed alum and salt, I experienced a sensation of coldness, and with it—the alum and salt—I cured the torment of the toothache.

How to Stop the Flow of Blood.

Housekeepers, mechanics, and others, in handling tools, knives and other sharp instruments, very frequently receive severe cuts, from which blood flows profusely and oftentimes endangers life itself. Blood may be made to cease flowing as follows: Take the fine dust of tea and bind it to the wound—at all times accessible and easily obtained. After the blood has ceased to flow, laudanum may be advantageously applied to the wound. Due regard to these instructions would save agitation of mind, and running for the surgeon, who would probably make no better prescription if he were present.

Application for Burns and Scalds.

Mix thoroughly together equal parts of the white of eggs and linseed or sweet oil; apply to the parts affected linen cloths saturated with this mixture, and change them as often as they become hot and uncomfortable. If linseed or sweet oil is not at hand, use molasses instead, till oil can be obtained. This application is only to be used in scalds and burns where the skin is off. In all cases where the skin is not removed, cloths wet every five minutes in a mixture made of two parts cold water, with one part common spirits, and applied, will be of more service. Continue these applications till the burning and inflammation are removed, then an ointment made of equal parts beeswax, fresh butter, and resin, melted together, will soon heal the sores and remove the scars. Burns and scalds must always be kept excluded from the light and air as much as possible, as this increases the irritation and prevents their rapid healing.

To Destroy Flies.

To one pint milk add a quarter pound of raw sugar, two ounces of ground pepper; simmer them together eight or ten minutes, and place it about in shallow dishes. The flies attack it readily, and are soon suffocated. By this method kitchens, &c., may be kept clear of flies all summer, without the danger attending poison.

Ladies' Fire-Proof Dresses.

Within a very short time two young ladies have been burnt to death, owing to their light muslin dresses catching fire from a lucifer match—one in London, the other in Colchester. It ought to be generally known that all ladies' light dresses may be made fire-proof at a mere nominal cost, by steeping them, or the linen or cotton used in making them, in a diluted solution of chloride of zinc. We have seen the very finest cambric so prepared held in the flame of a candle, and charred to dust without the least flame; and we have been informed that since Clara Webster, a dancer, was burnt to death, from her clothes catching fire on the stage, the muslin dresses of all the dancers at the best theaters are made fire-proof. Our manufacturers should take the hint.

Superior Black Writing Ink.

Take powdered nutgalls, four ounces; gum arabic, one ounce; sulphate of iron, two ounces; cold rain water, five teacupfuls. Mix, and bottle. Shake them once a day for three weeks, then strain through a flannel cloth. This forms the best and most durable black ink in use. It never fades or becomes moldy. Black ink should never be boiled, as heat destroys the coloring principle and renders it transient and pale.

How to Make Blacking.

Take of ivory black and treacle each twelve ounces, spermaceti oil four ounces, white wine vinegar four pints. Mix. This blacking, recommended by Mr. Gray, lecturer on the *materia medica*, is superior in giving leather a finer polish than any of those that are advertised, as they all contain sulphuric acid (oil of vitriol), which is necessary to give it the polishing quality, but it renders leather rotten and very liable to crack.

How to Make Temperance Beer.

Take three pounds of brown sugar, with one and a half pints of molasses, four ounces tartaric acid, two teaspoonfuls of essence of sassafras; mix in two quarts of boiling water, strain it and cool, when it is fit for use. Take two tablespoonfuls for a tumbler two-thirds full of water, add a half teaspoonful of soda. You will find it a cooling and delightful beverage for summer.

And here is a recipe for making cream beer:

To one gallon of warm water take two tablespoonfuls of tartaric acid, one bowl of good brown or coffee sugar, two tablespoonfuls of ginger, and one cup of yeast. Let it stand over night, and it is fit for use by adding a small quantity of soda as you drink it. Try this, and see if you do not call it good.

Apple Jelly.

Pare, quarter, and completely remove the core of the apples, and put in a pot, without water, closely covered, and put into an oven or over the fire. When pretty well stewed, the juice is to be squeezed out through a cloth, to which a little white of an egg is added, and then the sugar; skim it previous to boiling, and then reduce it to a proper consistency, and an excellent jelly will be the product.

To Take Out Mildew.

Mix soft-soap with starch powdered, half as much salt and the juice of a lemon; lay it on the part, on both sides, with a brush. Let it lie on the grass day and night till the stain comes out.

Cure for Stammering.

Those afflicted with this annoyance, at every syllable pronounced must tap at the same time with the finger. By so doing the most inveterate stammerer will be surprised to find he can pronounce quite fluently; and by long and constant practice he will pronounce perfectly well. This may be explained in two ways, either by a sympathetic consentaneous action of the nerves of voluntary motion in the finger, and in those of the tongue, which is the most probable; or it may be that the movement of the finger distracts the attention of the individual from his speech, and allows a free action of the nerves concerned in articulation.

To Clean Black Silks.

To bullock's gall add boiling water sufficient to make it warm, and with a clean sponge rub the silk well on both sides, squeeze it well out, and proceed again in like manner. Rinse it in spring water, and change the water till perfectly clean ; dry it in the air, and pin it out on a table ; but first dip the sponge in glue-water, and rub it on the wrong side ; then dry it before a fire.

Thirst Worse than Hunger.

That disturbance of the general system which is known under the name of " Raging Thirst," is far more terrible than that of starvation, and for this reason : During absence from food the organism can still live upon its own substance, which furnishes all the necessary material; but during abstinence from liquid the organism has no such source of supply within itself. Men have been known to endure absolute privation of food for some weeks; but three days of absolute privation of drink (unless in a moist atmosphere) is perhaps the limit of endurance. Thirst is the most atrocious torture ever invented. It is that which most effectually tames animals. Mr. Astley, when he had a refractory horse, always used thirst as the most effective power of coercion, giving a little water as a reward for every act of obedience.

To Dip Rusty Black Silks.

If it requires to be red-dyed, boil logwood; and in half an hour put in the silk, and let it simmer half an hour. Take it out, and dissolve a little blue vitriol and green copperas ; cool the copper; let it simmer half an hour, then dry it over a stick in the air. If not red-dyed, pin it out, and rinse it in spring water, in which half a teaspoonful of oil of vitriol has been put. Work it about five minutes, rinse it in cold water, and finish it by pinning and rubbing it with gum water.

Curious Mode of Silvering Ivory.

Immerse a small slip of ivory in a weak solution of nitrate of silver, and let it remain till the solution has given it a deep yellow color; then take it out and immerse it in a tumbler of clear water, and expose it, in the water, to the rays of the sun. In about three hours the ivory acquires a black color; but the black surface, on being rubbed, soon becomes changed to a brilliant silver.

To Make Red Sealing Wax.

Take of shell-lac, well powdered, two parts, of resin and vermilion, powdered, each one part. Mix them well together and melt them over a gentle fire, and when the ingredients seem thoroughly incorporated, work the wax into sticks. Where shell-lac cannot be procured, seed-lac may be substituted for it.

The quantity of vermilion may be diminished without any injury to the sealing wax, where it is not required to be of the highest and brightest red color; and the resin should be of the whitest kind, as that improves the effect of the vermilion.

Sea-Sickness Curable.

I am much surprised at the opinion which is so prevalent of the utter incurability of sea-sickness. I believe this opinion to exist among the non-medical part of the community from sheer ignorance, and amongst sea-going surgeons from a supineness in applying remedies—a fault to which they are rather too subject. In the greater number of instances I allow the stomach to discharge its contents once or twice, and then, if there is no organic disease, I give five drops of chloroform in a little water, and, if necessary, repeat the dose in four or six hours. The almost constant effect of this treatment, if conjoined with a few simple precautions, is to cause an immediate sensation, as it were, of warmth in the stomach, accompanied by almost total relief of the nausea and sickness, likewise curing the distressing headache, and usually causing a quiet sleep, from which the passenger awakes quite well.

Balsamic and Anti-Putrid Vinegar.

Take rue, sage, mint, rosemary, and lavender, fresh gathered, of each a handful, cut them small, and put them in a stone jar; pour upon the herbs a pint of the best white-wine vinegar; cover the jar close, and let it stand eight days in the sun, or near the fire; then strain it off, and dissolve it in an ounce of camphor. This liquid, sprinkled about the sick chamber, or fumigated, will much revive the patient, and prevent the attendants from receiving infection.

To Make Ink for Printing on Linen with Types.

Dissolve one part of asphaltum in four parts of oil of turpentine, and add lamp-black, or black-lead, in fine powder, in sufficient quantity to render the ink of a proper consistence for printing with types.

To Clean Gold Lace.

Gold lace is easily cleaned and restored to its original brightness by rubbing it with a soft brush dipped in roche alum, burnt, sifted to a very fine powder.

To Clean China and Glass.

The best material for cleaning either porcelain or glassware is fuller's earth, but it must be beaten into a fine powder and carefully cleared from all rough or hard particles, which might endanger the polish of the brilliant surface.

To Explore Unventilated Places.

Light some sheets of brown paper and throw into the well or cavern; also, fix a long pipe to a pair of bellows, and blow for some time into the place.

Black Sealing Wax.

Proceed as directed for the red wax, only instead of the vermilion substitute the best ivory black.

Green Sealing Wax.

Proceed as in the black; only instead of vermilion use verdigris powdered; or, where the color is required to be bright, distilled or crystals of verdigris.

Blue Sealing Wax.

As the above; only changing the vermilion for smalt well powdered; or, for a light blue, verditer may be used; as may, also, with more advantage, a mixture of both.

Yellow Sealing Wax.

As the above; only substituting masticot; or where a bright color is desired, turpeth mineral, instead of the vermilion.

Purple Sealing Wax.

As the red; only changing half the quantity of vermilion for an equal or greater proportion of smalt, according as the purple is desired to be bluer or redder.

Uncolored Soft Sealing Wax.

Take of bees' wax 1 lb., turpentine 8 oz., and olive oil 1 oz. Place them in a proper vessel over the fire, and let them boil for some time, and the wax will be then fit to be formed into rolls or cakes for use.

Red, Black, Green, Blue, Yellow, and Purple Soft Sealing Wax.

Add to the preceding composition, while boiling, an ounce or more of any ingredients directed above for coloring the hard sealing wax; and stir the matter well about, till the color be thoroughly mixed with the wax.

The proportion of the coloring ingredients may be increased, if the color produced by that here given be not found strong enough.

Blackberry Wine.

There is no wine equal to the blackberry wine, when properly made, either in flavor or for medical purposes, and all persons who can conveniently do so, should manufacture enough for their own use every year, as it is invaluable in sickness as a tonic, and nothing is a better remedy for bowel diseases. We therefore give the receipt for making it, and, having tried it ourselves, we speak advisedly on the subject: Measure your berries and bruise them; to every gallon adding on a quart of boiling water. Let the mixture stand twenty-four hours, stirring occasionally; then strain off the liquor into a cask, to every gallon adding two pounds of sugar, cork tight, and let it stand till the following October, and you will have wine ready for use, without further straining or boiling, that will make lips smack that never smacked under similar influences before.

To Prepare Waterproof Boots.

Boots and shoes may be rendered impervious to water by the following composition: Take three ounces of spermaceti, and melt it in a pipkin or other earthen vessel over a slow fire; add thereto six drachms of India rubber, cut into slices, and these will presently dissolve. Then add, *seriatim*, of tallow eight ounces, hog's lard two ounces, amber varnish four ounces. Mix, and it will be fit for use immediately. The boots or other material to be treated are to receive two or three coats, with a common blacking brush, and a fine polish is the result.

To Make Leather and other Articles Waterproof.

Dissolve ten pounds of India rubber, cut into bits, the smaller the better, in twenty gallons of pure spirits of turpentine, by putting them together into a tin vessel that will hold forty gallons. This vessel is to be immersed in *cold* water, contained in a boiler, to which fire is to be applied so as to make the *water* boil, occasionally supplying what is lost by evaporation. Here it is to remain until a perfect solution of the caoutchouc in the turpentine is obtained. One hundred and fifty pounds of *pure* bees' wax are now to be dissolved in one hundred gallons of pure spirits of turpentine, to which add twenty pounds of Burgundy pitch and ten pounds of gum frankincense. The solution to be obtained as directed for the caoutchouc. Mix the two solutions, and, when cold, add ten gallons of copal varnish, and put the whole into a reservoir, diluting it with one hundred gallons of lime water, five gallons at a time, and stirring it well up for six or eight hours in succession, which stirring must be repeated when any of the composition is taken out. If it is wanted black, mix twenty pounds of lamp-black with twenty gallons of turpentine (which twenty gallons should be deducted from the quantity previously employed) and add it previously to putting in the lime water.

To use it, lay it on the leather with a painter's brush, and rub it in.

To Clean Silk Stockings.

Wash with soap and water ; and simmer them in the same for ten minutes, rinsing in cold water. For a blue cast, put one drop of liquid blue into a pan of cold spring water, run the stockings through this a minute or two, and dry them For a pink cast, put one or two drops of saturated pink dye into cold water, and rinse them through this. For a flesh color, add a little rose pink in a thin soap liquor, rub them with a clean flannel, and calender or mangle them.

To Avoid Injury from Bees.

A wasp or bee swallowed may be killed before it can do harm, by taking a teaspoonful of common salt dissolved in water. It kills the insect, and cures the sting.

To Stop Cracks in Chimneys.

To stop cracks in chimneys and stoves, the insertion of stove pipes, open joints in pipes, and all places of the kind : dissolve common salt in water—as much as the water will take up—and thicken it with clean ashes till it becomes a mortar of temper for working. This will harden in a short time to a firm cement, and is better than mortar for the purpose mentioned, and can always be easily obtained.

Care of Stoves and Pipes.

When stoves are no longer needed, they are quite frequently set aside in an out-building, or other out-of-the-way place, with no further thought until again wanted for use. If neglected, the rust of the summer may injure them more than the whole winter's wear, particularly the parts made of sheet iron. They should be kept as free from dampness as possible, and occasionally cleaned if rust be observed, It is best to apply a coating of linseed oil to the pipes before putting them away. It should be done while the pipes are warm (not hot), and keep at a low temperature five or six hours. This is said to impart a fine luster, and prevent rusting.

Medical Uses of Salt.

In many cases of disordered stomach a teaspoonful of salt is a certain cure for colic. Put a teaspoonful of salt in a pint of cold water, drink it, and go to bed. The same will revive a person who has had a heavy fall. In an apoplectic fit no time should be lost in pouring down salt and water if the patient swallow, if not, the head must be sponged with cold water until the sense returns, when salt will completely restore the patient from lethargy. Salt will expel worms if used in food in moderate quantities. It aids digestion. Much salt meat is injurious.

Wall Paper.

To clean wall paper use wheat bran.

All Letters for Prof. Hamilton should be addressed thus:

R. L. HAMILTON, M.D.,
Post Office Box No. 4952,
NEW YORK CITY.

www.ingramcontent.com/pod-product-compliance
Lightning Source LLC
Chambersburg PA
CBHW032147010726
47493CB00008BA/2618